The Elephant of Surprise

The Russel Middlebrook Series, Book 4

Brent Hartinger

Buddha Kitty Books

For Michael Jensen
And for Harold Hartinger

Two men who both
still know how to surprise me

PREVIOUSLY

The Elephant of Surprise is the fourth book in the Russel Middlebrook Series, the story of a gay teenager named Russel and his collection of friends, especially Min, who is bisexual, and Gunnar, who is straight.

In **Geography Club**, the first book in the series, Russel and Min create a secret gay group at their school, which they call the Geography Club, thinking it sounds so boring no straight person will join. One of the members is Kevin, a popular jock, who Russel begins dating. But when Min suggests they ask Brian Bund, the school outcast and a rumored gay kid, to join their group, the issue splits the membership. Kevin especially wants to keep the club as secret as possible. The disagreement causes the Geography Club to implode. Russel is outed, and Kevin doesn't stand up for him. Kevin eventually apologizes, but it's too late:

Russel decides he doesn't love Kevin anymore.

In *The Order of the Poison Oak*, the second book in the series, Russel, Min, and Gunnar get jobs working as counselors at a summer camp for burn survivors. After competing with Min for a guy named Web, Russel eventually begins a relationship with another counselor, a burn survivor named Otto Digmore. Meanwhile, Gunnar also ends up in a relationship, with a girl named Em. Russel and Otto spend a happy summer together, but must then return to their homes, eight hundred miles apart.

In the third book in the series, *Double Feature: Attack of the Soul-Sucking Brain Zombies/Bride of the Soul-Sucking Brain Zombies* (also sold under the title *Split Screen*), Russel, Min, and Gunnar get jobs as zombie extras in a horror film being filmed in their area. We then see the events of the following week from two different perspectives: Russel's and Min's.

In *Attack of the Soul-Sucking Brain Zombies*, Russel's version, Otto, Russel's long-distance boyfriend, comes for a visit. At the same time, Kevin reappears in his life, apologizing for past misdeeds and hinting he wants to get back together. Russel eventually makes the decision to stay with Otto. He meets Kevin in a park at night to tell him the choice he's made and is shocked to see Kevin hooking up with an older man. Russel confronts him, but Kevin acts like an arrogant jerk. Russel is more certain than ever he was right to choose Otto.

In **Bride of the Soul-Sucking Brain Zombies**, Min's version of this same period of time, Min falls for a new girl, Leah, despite the fact that Leah is closeted. They begin dating. Meanwhile, the same night that Russel confronts Kevin in the park at night, Min meets Kevin first. She lays into him, telling him he had his chance with Russel before and he screwed it up, and he's going to ruin Russel's new chance for happiness with Otto. Tearfully, Kevin agrees. In other words, the "older man" Russel saw that night in the park was merely Min hugging Kevin in the dark. Min listens in the bushes while Russel confronts Kevin. Kevin is a total jerk to Russel, but Min knows he's only pretending in order to get Russel to hate him so he can move on with Otto. Min finally sees just how much Kevin truly loves Russel. But she also knows that Russel has chosen to be with Otto, and that for the time being, she must keep Kevin's noble actions in the park a secret.

CHAPTER ONE

I was deep in the thick of the jungle, wild animals glaring at me from all around. I stood frozen, certain that if I made even the slightest move, these vicious beasts would lunge for me, biting with glistening fangs and rending my flesh with razor claws.

No, really, I was!

I know, I know. You're thinking: "He always does this. He starts the story pretending he's in the middle of some exciting event—a war, a fire, a zombie apocalypse—but then it just turns out to be something *metaphorical*. I'm not falling for it this time."

But this time, I really *was* in the middle of a jungle. I really *was* surrounded by vicious, wild animals.

Okay, so it was just the "African safari" section of the zoo. The "jungle" was the bamboo and banana plants growing along the concrete pathways, and the "wild animals" were in the enclosures all around me—the "immersion" kind, designed to recreate the animals' natural habitat, but with cleverly disguised moats and hidden wire fences keeping the lions and hyenas and wildebeests away from all the helpless people.

But hey, at least it's not a metaphor for anything!

My name is Russel Middlebrook, I'm seventeen years old and a junior in high school, and I'd come to the zoo on a Saturday afternoon with my two best friends, Min and Gunnar—although Gunnar had wandered off somewhere else at that exact moment.

"Did you know that lions are the only species of cat where the males and females look different?" Min said, staring out at the animals.

I hadn't known that. There was a lot I didn't know, something I was reminded of whenever I spent any time around Min, a self-described "Chow Mein brain." This is my polite way of saying that—at least in a certain light and from a certain angle—Min can be something of a know-it-all.

"They act differently too," she said. "The females don't just raise the young, they also do most of the hunting. The males look and act all regal, and they're big on fighting each other, but they're mostly sort of worthless." At this, she sort of eyed me pointedly.

"Wait," I said. "What was that look for?"

"What look?"

"You just sort of eyed me, as though the way male lions act is somehow a reflection on me, on males in general."

"I did not."

"You totally did! That's totally sexist. You of all people. I can't believe how sexist that is!" For the record, Min is an outspoken feminist (I am too).

She ignored me, just turned for the wildebeests. (Or wildebeest? Does anyone know the plural of "wildebeest"?) Out in their immersion pen, five of the animals stood listlessly in the dirt—their hooves had long since worn the grass down to almost nothing. So much for recreating their natural habitat.

"As for the wildebeest"—naturally, Min knew the plural of wildebeest—"people talk about herd animals like they're mindless, that the 'herd mentality' is just everyone blindly following everyone else. But herds can actually be intelligent. Scientists now refer to it as something called 'swarm intelligence.'"

Min was being even more know-it-all-y than usual today. This had the effect of making *me* feel even more insecure than usual.

"What's the only marsupial where both sexes have a pouch?" I said.

She looked at me. "What?"

"Marsupials. You know: animals with pouches—like kangaroos and koala bears."

"I know what a marsupial is," Min said.

"The water opossum. That's the only one where both the males and females have pouches. Well, I guess male Tasmanian tigers also had pouches, but they're supposed to be extinct."

She kept staring at me. "What exactly does that have to do with anything?"

"Well, you were just talking about how male and female lions were different. And about how wildebeests—I mean wilde*beest*—use swarm intelligence."

"Yes, but that's because we were looking at lions and wildebeest. We're not looking at water opossums. I mean, this is the African savannah. Aren't water opossums from Mexico?"

Were they? I didn't know. I'd only known that bit about male water opossums having pouches from a special on TV a few nights before, but I didn't remember the narrator saying where they lived. So not only did Min know more than I did about every other animal, she even knew more than I did about the one animal that I'd thought I'd known something about.

She smirked. "Feeling a little insecure today, are we?"

I've already admitted that if Min could be something of a know-it-all, I could be a little insecure—at least in a certain light and from a certain angle.

"What about you?" I said.

"What about me?" she said.

"Something's up. What's going on?" I couldn't come right out and accuse Min of being more know-it-all-y than usual, but it was kind of implied.

She turned and headed into this fake cave-tunnel that led to the next cluster of animal displays. I followed. Inside the cavern, there was this stretch of glass panels that showed African termites in their nest, sort of like a giant ant farm. I think the idea was that we were supposed to be walking through one of those giant termite mounds you see on the African savannah. It wasn't bad, actually.

Min lingered at the termite display. Behind the glass, termites plodded. They're slower than ants: they don't scurry.

"It's Leah," she said.

Min is bisexual, and Leah was her girlfriend who went to a different school. It was February, and the two of them had been going out forever, at least since November.

"What about her?" I said, concerned.

"She's hiding something from me. Keeping secrets."

This bears some explanation. Back in November, when Min and Leah had first started going out, they'd had this big conflict because Leah didn't want to come out as a lesbian, at least not in high school. Leah knew she was a lesbian—she wasn't conflicted or "questioning"—but she also wanted a "normal" high school experience. She just didn't want to have to stand up for herself or be the center of attention. For a time, this had been a real sore point for Min because (a) she's definitely a stand-up-for-yourself kind of person, and (b) she'd gone through this disastrous relationship earlier last year with this girl who refused to come out, and Min had vowed never to do anything like that again. But eventually Min had come around to the idea that different people, even people who like each other, can sometimes come to different conclusions about things.

"How do you know?" I said to Min, about the secrets Leah was supposedly keeping.

"Little things. Like she's weird about letting me borrow her phone. And she changes the subject whenever I talk about the future."

"You could be imagining things," I said.

"I know. It's mostly just a feeling."

I spotted something on the floor of the fake cave: a dead termite. Was it possible one of them had escaped from the colony? And if one of them had escaped, did that mean one of the lions or hyenas or tigers could get out of their cages too? Hey, maybe I really was in danger of being torn apart by a wild animal.

"How's the relationship itself?" I asked.

"That's just it. I thought we were doing great. But suddenly it feels like she's withdrawn. I mean, she's not here today, is she?"

"But maybe she's just reacting to your being suspicious."

"I know." She sighed. "Do you think she could be cheating? Like, with a boyfriend or something? I mean, isn't that part of the 'normal' high school experience?"

I thought about this. I was tempted to say, "No

way! Never!" But I'd had an experience of my own back in November when I'd learned something about my ex, a guy named Kevin Land, that had totally shocked me. Now I knew you couldn't ever assume anything about anyone.

So finally, I just said, "I don't know. I don't think so, but I'm not sure I know anything anymore."

Min gave me a long look, like she wanted to say something, but didn't quite know what. Finally, she turned and walked the rest of the way through the termite mound out into the daylight of the next cluster of displays: zebras, elephants, and monkeys. You expect monkeys to be swinging around and whooping it up, don't you? These weren't. Maybe it was too cold that time of year. What were they doing putting animals from the African savannah outside in February anyway? Besides, those monkeys were in cages. How excited could they ever be?

"How are things with Otto?" Min said as we stopped to watch the monkeys.

Otto was my boyfriend—a really great guy. We'd been going out even longer than forever, since summer the year before when we'd met at camp. Unfortunately, he lived eight hundred miles away.

But how *were* things with him? I had to think about that. It was right then I noticed the air smelled like three different kinds of animal shit.

"Things are good, I guess," I said. "Wait, no, they're great. No, hold on, maybe they're just good."

The last time I'd seen Otto, back in November, Min had been trying to figure out if she and Leah could be together, and I'd been trying to figure out if Otto and I could make a long-distance relationship work. In the end, we'd decided we could. And we had. That wasn't what was wrong. But something was. Did my feelings toward Otto have something to do with the fact that I'd been feeling especially insecure that day?

Min and I sighed at exactly the same time.

We looked at each other and laughed. It was one of those unexpected moments where you feel totally connected to the person next to you—sharing the exact same feeling in the exact same moment in time. Better still, you know it.

"Can I be totally honest?" I said.

"No," Min said. "Whatever gave you the idea you could be totally honest with me?"

I smiled. "I think I just feel like I'm in a bit of a rut. You know? I mean, I go to school and stare at screens and blackboards. I go home and stare at televisions and computer screens."

"And right now, Otto is nothing but a blip on one of those computer screens."

"Yes. No. Maybe. It's more than that. But yeah, with our relationship being an online one, I guess everything does seem a little predictable. There's no excitement. No adventure. How could there be? We're in completely different states!"

Now we'd finally gotten to the bottom of it: Min and I, the know-it-all and the insecure neurotic, were both feeling weirdness about our partners.

Over in one of the enclosures, a zebra shuffled its feet.

Relationships are tough, I thought. Who'd have thought that after all that drama with my ex, I'd miss it with Otto on any level? I guess it just goes to show that when it comes to relationships, you can never predict what's waiting for you up ahead. There are always dangers lurking, just out of sight. The whole experience was like being lost in a...

Oh, damn. I guess that whole jungle/wild animal thing is turning out to be a pretty good metaphor after all. Sorry about that! (Which isn't to say the "wild" animals were playing their parts. Would it have killed them to be a little less listless? For one of the lions to let out a terrifying roar behind us?)

At least I wasn't lost in the metaphorical jungle alone. I had Min, and she had me, and together we had our other best friend Gunnar. We'd forge our way through the metaphorical termite mounds together.

It was at that exact moment that Gunnar, in fact, finally reappeared. Hippopotamus ears sprouted from his tousled head—a headband of some sort, probably from the gift shop—but he had his face in his phone.

"Gunnar!" I said. I was always happy to see him—even after all these years as best friends, even after only being separated for fifteen minutes.

He looked up. "What's gnu?" he said.

"What?" I said.

"Gnu is another name for wildebeest," Min said.

I should explain (Gunnar always takes a little explaining). If Min is a know-it-all and I'm insecure, Gunnar is…different. Quirky. Take the hippopotamus ears. Was he being hipster-ironic? Geek-chic? Or just kind of clueless?

That's the thing with Gunnar: you never really know. That's also what's so great about him. It's not that he doesn't care what other people think of him—sometimes he *does* care, desperately. He just can't ever do anything about it. He is too different to even realize how different he is, if that makes any sense. It's something of a curse, but it's a good curse: it makes him one of the most interesting people I've ever met, and probably one of the most interesting people I ever *will* meet.

"Oh!" he said suddenly. "A pissing zebra!" With his phone, he immediately took a photo of the zebra and posted it to his online profile.

Okay, once again, I need to explain something Gunnar-related: a couple of weeks earlier, he had announced to both Min and me one day at lunch: "I've decided to chronicle my entire life, every waking second of every day, online for the whole world to see."

"How is that different from any other teenager?" Min had said.

"Mostly, it's a question of degree," Gunnar had

said. "Plus, I'm doing the whole thing ironically." He'd been typing into his phone even as we'd talked.

"You just recorded that conversation of you telling us what you're doing, and you're now posting it online, aren't you?" I'd said.

"Yup," Gunnar had said. And I'd known right then that, as much as I like Gunnar and am always happy to see him, this was going to be his most annoying obsession yet.

Back at the zoo, I didn't bother filling Gunnar in on the conversation Min and I had just had. He wasn't really the kind of guy you had conversations about your love life with (although sometimes he surprised me with how much he picked up on the things going on around him).

"Where to now?" I said.

Min and I looked around the zoo. Gunnar, meanwhile, took a picture of an ant trying to lift a huge piece of a cinnamon churro.

"I think I'm ready to go," Min said.

"Yeah," I said. "I'm just not feeling the zoo either."

"I don't think I like zoos in general," Min said. "It seems cruel to put wild animals in cages, then use them for our entertainment. But even as entertainment, they're just not that interesting. They're boring. There's no element of surprise."

Gunnar looked up. "Elephant of Surprise?"

"*Element* of surprise," Min said.

I laughed, and Gunnar did too. Okay, so he didn't

always surprise me with how much he picked up on the things going on around him.

"What?" Min said.

"I really thought that's what you said!" Gunnar said happily, even as he was posting something about it online. "The Elephant of Surprise! I mean, this is a zoo, right? We're standing next to the elephants."

Min smiled at last. "The Elephant of Surprise. Can you imagine if it really existed? No, I definitely think we can do without him—or her."

"Yeah," Gunnar said. "Imagine if he stepped on you. Ouch!"

Looking back now, I can see we were all wrong about that elephant not existing. There definitely is such a creature, and it was definitely on the move in all three of our lives.

Oh, and Gunnar was right: when the Elephant of Surprise stepped on you, it really, really hurt.

CHAPTER TWO

That night, I IMed Otto, the boyfriend who lived 800 miles away. FYI: my screen name is "Smuggler." His is, well, obvious:

Smuggler: Hello you.

OttoManEmpire: Hello you.

Smuggler: How was your day?

OttoManEmpire: Eh. But it's nice to talk to you.

Smuggler: It's nice to talk to you too.

This was all true. I felt so safe around Otto,

because I could always be exactly who I was. I hesitate to say this because I know how annoying it will sound, but at this point in our relationship, Otto and I had become one of those couples who had a way of always knowing exactly what the other was thinking. Weirdly, the effect even worked over IM.

Smuggler: Did you know that lions are the only species of cat where the male and female don't look basically the same?

OttoManEmpire: What'd you do, go to the zoo today with Min?

Smuggler: LOL! That's it EXACTLY!

See what I mean? It was uncanny.

I told him more about my trip to the zoo, sans the discussion Min and I had had about being vaguely dissatisfied with our partners, and he told me about going shopping with his mom (it wasn't as boring as it sounds—he found a wallet with fifty dollars in it).

Smuggler: You know what? I like you. You're a good friend.

OttoManEmpire: I totally agree.

But.

Wait. Why was there a "but" there? Was it because something felt off? It wasn't just a conservation between Min and me at the zoo. Something had been off for a while now. But I couldn't put my finger on exactly what it was.

I waited for Otto to type something. After all, if we always knew what the other one was thinking, maybe he could tell me what I was thinking about our relationship, since *I* apparently didn't know.

OttoManEmpire: What's wrong?

I knew exactly what he meant: not what's wrong with me. What was wrong with us.

Smuggler: I honestly don't know.

This whole conservation had this weird feeling of anticipation to it, like right before you leave the house on a trip to somewhere you've never been. You know *something* is going to happen, but you have no real idea what, and it's a little scary, but also kind of exciting. What unexpected destination was this conversation going to take us to?

Smuggler: You're my friend. One of my best friends. And you always will be.

OttoManEmpire: But.

Once again, Otto was reading my thoughts. But he didn't seem to know what I was thinking any more than I did.

Smuggler: We're friends.

OttoManEmpire: But not boyfriends.

That was it! He'd said exactly what I was feeling, even though I hadn't known I was feeling it.

Wait. Otto and I were breaking up?

OttoManEmpire: No, we're not breaking up.

Smuggler: We're not?

OttoManEmpire: Okay, maybe we are. But I think maybe we already did. At some point back and we just didn't realize it.

Was this true? Had we gone from boyfriends to good friends and not even known it? It felt true.

Smuggler: Are you sad?

Otto didn't type anything for a second.

OttoManEmpire: Yes. No. Maybe.

Smuggler: Me too. Well, a little sad, but not too bad.

OttoManEmpire: And a little excited too.

Smuggler: Excited? Why?

OttoManEmpire: Well, there's this guy I know.

Wait. Otto had a crush on someone else?

OttoManEmpire: It's not like it sounds. It's not like I've been thinking about this.

But here's the really interesting part: I wasn't jealous. In fact, I was kind of excited for him.

Which told me everything I needed to know. Somewhere along the way, we really had gone from being boyfriends to good friends. It had something to do with what I'd been telling Min at the zoo. It's one thing to feel safe in the wild jungle safari of your relationship—to know the other person is watching your back for lions and tigers. It's something else entirely to be bored.

I didn't tell Min and Gunnar what had happened until I saw them in the school hallway Monday morning before class. All around us, locker doors squealed and slammed. The air smelled like hair product and soap from all the early morning showers, with a faint hint of ammonia from the floor.

"Remember the Elephant of Surprise?" I said to my two friends, standing by our own lockers. "He stopped by Saturday night."

"What?" Min said. "How so?"

I explained how Otto and I had broken up, not because of the long-distance thing, but because we'd both basically realized at the same time that we'd somehow stopped being "lovers" and turned into "friends."

"And you didn't call me?" she said.

"No," I said. "But that's kinda the point. It just wasn't that big a deal."

"Russel, I'm sorry."

"I'm okay. Really."

"But it's not like he's gone forever, right?" Gunnar said. "I mean, you guys are still friends?"

"Yeah, definitely," I said. "And I'm not just saying that. That's the whole point: we *are* friends. Really, really good friends. But we're not boyfriends."

"Good," Gunnar said. "I really like Otto."

As we were talking, Kevin Land, my ex, stepped into sight at the far end of the hall. He was wearing a blue sweatshirt (spattered with red paint) and carrying a computer bag instead of a backpack. It's not like he was in my direct line-of-sight or anything. No, he was buried somewhere within the crush of people. But I guess you could say that I tended to be aware of exactly where he was and exactly what he was doing whenever he was around.

Oh, God, Kevin Land. How do I bullet-point this to make it as simple as possible for those who are just joining the story now?

- He's totally hot.
- We'd had a thing almost a year before. But he was closeted, and a total jerk about it, so it hadn't worked out.
- Then, in the fall, he'd come crawling back, desperate to make amends, even coming out to his friends. I'd almost given into him when I learned he was even more of a jerk than I'd thought before.

And before you call me a hypocrite for saying I was totally done with him, but was still obviously aware of his every move, let me just say I knew it was a problem and was working on it. But come on: I'm only human—a teenager in high school, no less. Isn't this when you're allowed to do dumb, hypocritical things like this?

Kevin yanked on the padlock on his locker, but it didn't open. Had he dialed the wrong combination?

I deliberately turned away. "I'm done with love," I said to Min and Gunnar.

Min looked up from her locker. Gunnar glanced

up from his phone.

"What?" she said.

"I mean it," I said. "After that whole thing last year and now this thing with Otto, I'm done. At least for a while."

"Don't bother," Gunnar said. "I tried that last summer at camp. Remember? Em and I got together anyway." Em was Gunnar's girlfriend. She went to another school in town, but she was so great she was even humoring him on his annoying document-his-entire-life-online obsession. "Love will always find a way."

"Love can go fuck itself!" I said. I opened my locker, defiantly blocking any view of Kevin (even though I still somehow sensed that he'd opened his lock on the second try).

Gunnar just shook his head sadly. "You know, you're practically begging the universe for an ironic twist of fate."

"I am *not.*"

"You are. Now you have no choice but to fall in love with an ice sculpture."

"An ice sculpture?" I said, confused.

Gunnar shrugged. "Not only can it not love you back, it'll melt in a couple of hours anyway. I mean, talk about your tragic love affairs!"

"Really, Gunnar? Really?" I said this, but it was impossible not to laugh. Even Min laughed, and she had a habit of not laughing at Gunnar's weird jokes.

"The point is, you're just totally tempting fate," he said.

"I am not tempting fate." I looked at Min. "Help me out here."

"Hey, I'm with Gunnar on this one," she said.

"Okay, I'm tempting fate. But if tempting fate means that I'm forced to do whatever I vow not to do, then I also vow not to eat chocolate cake at every meal. And I vow *not* to have my parents give me my own car."

"You realize, of course, you're totally missing the point," Min said. "Right?"

"And *you* realize that fate doesn't really exist," I said. "Right?"

Min rolled her eyes. "It's a *metaphor*. About how crazy it is to think we can predict the future."

Another metaphor, huh? Well, as I've already made clear, I was feeling pretty done with metaphors.

So I ignored her.

"I vow *not* to sleep every day until noon!" I said. "I vow *not* to have my parents install a hot tub in our backyard!"

Gunnar looked up from his phone long enough to take a couple of steps back from me.

"What?" I said.

"Nothing," he said. "Just putting as much space as possible between me, and you and the universe."

* * *

Fate didn't strike me down the rest of the school day. Then again, if I were fate, I wouldn't have bothered with our stupid school in our boring backwater town either.

That day after school, Min and I lingered in the courtyard waiting for Gunnar, who was nearby taking a picture of a melting ice-cream bar. Once again, I was totally aware of the existence of Kevin Land, tying his shoes on the opposite side of the courtyard.

"How's Leah?" I said to Min. I'd been meaning to ask her that ever since we'd talked on Saturday.

"What?" she said. "Oh, she's fine." She fiddled with her hair, back to black now after she'd dyed it purple the year before.

I stared at Min. "No, seriously." Min, Gunnar, and I joked with and teased each other a lot, like that whole tempting fate thing in the hallway, but we all still cared about what was really going on.

"It's the same," she said. "I think something is up, but I have no idea what it is."

"Have you talked to her?" I said.

"Not yet." She thought for a second. "I think you should talk to Kevin."

"What?" I said, totally confused.

"Russel, you're checking him out even now. You're *always* checking him out."

I had been checking him out—he'd finished tying his shoes and was now texting someone—but had I really been that obvious?

"So what if I check him out?" I said. "We have a past."

"You and Otto have broken up now, so I think you should talk to him. Just talk."

"Min," I said. "*Why* would I talk to him? You know what he did!"

Remember when I'd said he'd done something that had totally shocked me? I'd arranged for us to meet at this park near my house, but when I'd got there, I'd seen him hooking up with an older guy in the bushes.

I repeat: *he was hooking up with a guy in the bushes while he was waiting to meet me!* Min was right that I couldn't predict the future, but I knew one thing for sure: there was no way Kevin Land was in mine.

"What'd I miss?" Gunnar said, having finished his latest update.

"Min wants me to talk to Kevin," I said. "Now that Otto and I have broken up."

"Seriously?" Gunnar said. "Why?"

"Because life is complicated," Min said. "Sometimes things aren't always black-and-white." *Min* was the one who was saying this? The bull-headed know-it-all who usually refused to compromise on anything? This was especially weird because Min had never liked Kevin, not since the very, very beginning.

"It's true, things aren't always black-and-white," I said. "But sometimes they are. And this is one of those times." I looked at Gunnar. "Let's go." He and I usually rode our bikes home from school together. Meanwhile, Min had her own car.

"Wait!" Min said, following behind us as we headed toward the bike rack. Naturally, it was located in just about the most unpleasant place on the whole campus: near the Dumpster behind the cafeteria. The whole area smelled incredibly foul, beyond sour. Even the asphalt around the Dumpster was sticky—the result of years of spills and leaks.

"Look," Min said to me, "there's something you need to know."

"No, there is *nothing* I need to know," I said. "Especially nothing about Kevin. I know what I need to know about him, which is that he's a total asshole."

"But—" Min said.

I stopped by the Dumpster. This was ironic: it was the same Dumpster where I'd once waited for Kevin, only to have him totally dog me in front of his friends. Talk about proving my point.

"Min?" I said. "Listen. I only broke up with Otto two days ago. The last thing in the world I want is to have anything to do with Kevin, now or ever. It's over. So whatever it is you have to say, don't say it."

It was at that exact moment that the heads of two people popped up out of the Dumpster next to us.

CHAPTER THREE

For a minute, I was confused. Had bullies thrown someone into the garbage? It wouldn't have been the first time.

But no. These were two people I didn't recognize: a guy and girl—teenagers, yes, but ones who didn't go to our school. It didn't look like they'd been *thrown* into the Dumpster—even now they weren't scrambling to get out. But why would anyone have gone in there voluntarily?

"Oh!" the girl said, like they hadn't known we were there. Like they hadn't wanted to be caught.

"Hey," the guy said, not sounding busted at all, but rather like we were greeting each other at a party.

"Um, hello," I said. "Did you lose something?"

"Nope," the guy said. "*Looking* for something."

"In the Dumpster?" But even as I said this, I knew: these were Dumpster divers. I'd seen homeless people rummage around in Dumpsters and trash cans before, but I didn't think I'd ever seen actual teenagers doing it.

I looked at Min, but her face was non-judgmental blank.

"Why not?" the girl said. "They just dumped the kitchen trash from lunch." She held up some kind of wrapped sandwich, still in its plastic wrap. "A lot of it's perfectly good."

"I wouldn't be so sure," I said. "If it came from our school lunchroom, it probably wasn't much good to begin with." I immediately felt stupid for saying this—for making a joke about how bad the food was in the school cafeteria when here were these people who were eating that same food after it had been tossed into the garbage.

But they both laughed, which I appreciated.

"You eat out of Dumpsters?" Gunnar said. He didn't sound judgmental either. It was more like he was just curious.

"Sometimes," the guy said, almost proudly—or maybe it was defiantly. "It's not like we take the half-eaten stuff that comes from the garbage cans or stuff that's been sitting in the sun. There really is a lot of stuff in here that's perfectly good—still wrapped, still cold. Schools and stuff are required by law to throw something out on a certain date. And sometimes they throw stuff out just because there's not enough room in the refrigerator."

"Are you homeless?" Gunnar said.

"Homeless by choice!" the girl said.

"Not really homeless," the guy said. "We're freegans."

"Freegans?" I said. Once again, I looked over at Min. If anyone would know what this was, she would. But her face was still blank—not non-judgmental blank now, more like she didn't know what a "freegan" was either. "What's that?" I asked the people in the Dumpster.

The guy climbed effortlessly up onto the metal rim, then hopped out. The girl followed him, almost as easily. Their backpacks bulged, no doubt with food from the Dumpster.

"I can't just tell you what a freegan is," he said. He smiled broadly. "That's something I definitely have to *show* you."

If I'd been alone, I wouldn't have gone with this guy—not in a million years. But since I was with Min and Gunnar, and since this guy and the girl were teenagers, my two friends and I sort of simultaneously decided, Well, why not? We didn't even talk about it—we just looked at each other and shrugged.

"Name's Wade," the guy said as he led us away.

"Venus," the girl said.

Min, Gunnar, and I gave them our names, but that's when I noticed that Wade and Venus weren't leading us out to the main road, which is where I was sort of expecting them to go, but rather to the back of the school, out by the sports fields—the track, the baseball diamond, and the football field.

Now that they were out of the Dumpster, I had a better look at both of them. Venus was tall and thin—at least as tall as Wade, maybe taller. Her clothes were all military green—one piece, like a flight suit—and her hair was mousy brown, which is maybe why she reminded me of a cattail. Or maybe it was the way she sort of swayed when she walked.

Wade was black. I didn't mention that before because I didn't want you making any assumptions—about a black guy in a Dumpster, I mean. He was wearing jeans and a jacket, but somehow (unlike Venus) they weren't dirty from the Dumpster—in fact, his white t-shirt looked spotless. He was also more solid than Venus. It was partly his body, which was a lot thicker than hers and looked to be about as hard as marble (they make black marble, right?). But it wasn't just that. He also had this serious, down-to-earth expression. His head was shaved shiny smooth, and his voice was deep and soothing. I liked that while he had testosterone to spare, there was still a gentleness to him—the kind of guy who studied ants as a kid, not tortured them with a magnifying glass.

He led us all right past the sports fields, to the big swath of vacant land behind the school. It was just a forgotten pine forest, mostly only used by the mountain bikers who'd carved dusty trails with their treads, and students taking a shortcut to school. It was only February, but there were already red ants on the ground, marching off to their anthills of twigs and needles. I couldn't imagine anything in here that Wade and Venus would want to show us. An abandoned car? Something in the grassy swamp on the far side of the woods?

"Where are you taking us?" Min asked.

"It's a surprise," Wade said, and you'd think this might have sounded scary or threatening, but it didn't, not at all.

Of course, me being me, this is when I realized that they were probably members of a cult, and they were leading us into the woods so someone else could drop burlap sacks over our heads, tie our hands and feet, and then carry us off to be brainwashed to worship turnips.

"Everyone's heard of dandelion tea and dandelion wine," Wade said, pointing to the weeds along the trail. "But did you know you can eat the entire plant? The flowers, the roots, the leaves—the leaves are a little bitter, but they're a really good source of calcium. And the seeds can be ground into flour. It's really kind of a perfect plant for foraging, because, well, they're everywhere, and there aren't any poisonous look-alikes. Everyone knows exactly what a dandelion looks like, right?"

The perfect plant for foraging? Why would anyone

want to forage? But then I reminded myself that I was talking to people who ate out of Dumpsters.

"There's so much you can eat that grows around here," Venus said. She pointed. "Even nettles! You can boil the roots and the leaves, and you can also eat the leaves on a young plant raw."

"They don't sting?" I said.

"They do! But only a little. That's what makes them fun—it's like a little tickle in your mouth. I only put a few nettle leaves in a wild greens salad anyway. If you ever come over to our place, I'll make you one, 'kay?"

I smiled. "Okay."

I looked over at Min for some kind of confirmation that Wade and Venus knew what the hell they were talking about—that they weren't planning on poisoning us with their nettles and dandelions. Min nodded once, signifying that, yeah, they were telling the truth.

For twenty minutes or so, we weaved our way through the woods, picking one trail over another. To tell the truth, I was growing increasingly excited— where exactly was Wade leading us?—so much so that I completely forgot to be worried that someone might be dropping a burlap sack over my head at any moment.

We smelled our destination before we saw it: a furious stench that was even more foul than the Dumpster back at the school.

The five of us came to a chain-link fence. Beyond the fence was a massive pit, maybe half a mile across, and the bottom of the pit was completely covered with garbage.

"The garbage dump?" Min said. "This is the big surprise?" Part of me saw her point. But another part of me wanted her to shut up. He hadn't shown us anything yet.

Wade said, "Just take a good look."

So we did. A gravel road wound down around the edge of the pit so garbage trucks could reach the level of the garbage itself. Meanwhile, once it was dumped, tractors covered the trash up with dirt, but over the years plenty of the garbage had fluttered free, especially paper, a layer of which had been caught at the base of the chain link fence, getting soggy in the rain, then hardening like papier-mâché into a strip along the ground like a baseboard. A huge flock of seagulls along with the occasional crow churned over the garbage like a swarm of giant flies.

Gunnar immediately started taking pictures with his phone.

"Americans produce fifteen hundred pounds of garbage each per year." It was actually Gunnar who said this, not Wade, even as he was focusing his phone-camera. "And most of that is just packaging— boxes and bags and containers for all the other stuff we buy."

"That's absolutely right!" Wade said. He sounded

positively gleeful, like Gunnar had just made his point for him. "And that doesn't include stuff we recycle—that takes a lot of energy too, just a little less of it—or sewage. Americans are five percent of the world's population, but we create forty percent of the world's garbage!"

"Incredible," I said, because it *was* incredible. By this point, I was already eating out of Wade's hand (presuming he cleaned it off it after climbing out of that Dumpster!).

"But what does this have to do with anything?" Min said, and it was all I could do not to scowl at her.

"Well, we're not done yet," Wade said. "There's still one other thing I want to show you."

He and Venus turned to lead us away, and Gunnar and I immediately followed. But Min didn't move from where she stood at that fence. I looked back at her.

I could see the open skepticism on her face. Unlike me, she was still expecting someone to drop a burlap sack over her head. And I guess she did have a point: what reason did we really have to go blithely on following this strange Pied Piper and his spacey girlfriend?

I stepped closer to her, even as Wade and Venus watched us from behind. "Let's just keep an open mind, okay?" When she didn't answer, I turned to Gunnar. "What do you want to do?"

Sure enough, he said, "I wanna know where this is going," just like I knew he would.

Finally, Min sighed, and we all stepped wordlessly into line behind Wade and Venus again.

We walked through the woods for another fifteen minutes or so. Once again, we smelled our destination before we actually saw it, and this time it smelled a lot better: woodsmoke coming from somewhere within the trees ahead of us.

A second later, we stepped out into a clearing. There was a cluster of tents—well, "tents" might be too strong a word. They were more like cardboard boxes and tarps arranged in such a way to provide cover from the rain. There was one actual tent, but it was dirty and frayed, with more duct tape than actual vinyl.

In the center of the clearing, a little bonfire conjured up the smoke we'd smelled. A cluster of people, mostly old men in flannel, sat around the fire on logs and in lawn furniture that was as pathetic as the tents. Truthfully, there were quite a few empty beer cans and bottles scattered around the campfire too—and most were of at least the sixteen-ounce variety.

"Wade!" said a man with almost no hair (or teeth).

"Hey, Myron," Wade said. "How you doin'?" At the same time, he opened his backpack and started passing out the sandwiches he'd collected from the Dumpster

"What is this place?" Gunnar said.

"A homeless camp," Venus said, opening her pack too.

Once again, Gunnar started taking pictures—no one seemed to mind, and a couple of the men mugged mercilessly.

Meanwhile, Min and I watched as Wade and Venus walked around the camp—well, Wade walked and Venus sort of floated. They gave out food: more sandwiches, a big tub of shredded cheese, some salads in plastic containers, and half a bag of English muffins.

Mostly, though, they just listened as the men talked to them, flirting with Venus and showing Wade things they'd collected in the woods.

One old man took off his shirt—he was crazy skinny—and Wade bent down behind him to examine his back. Even from where I was fifteen feet across the clearing, I caught a blast of the man's terrible body odor. But Wade, who was a lot closer, didn't seem to notice. He took a good look at an injury on the man's shoulder blade—a scary black fungus of some kind—and then I heard Wade saying something about a free clinic.

Truthfully, I was touched by his concern.

But Min was still sort of scowling. And when Wade returned to us, she said, "First you show us the garbage dump. Now this. Why?"

"Let's go somewhere where we can talk," he said, leading us off into the trees, like it would be rude to talk about anyone as if they were visual aids in a presentation, even homeless people.

Out of earshot, he and Venus faced us.

"You said you wanted to know what freeganism is," Wade said. "Well, freeganism is a movement that says there's something wrong with the world when we waste so much stuff, especially when there are so many people who have nothing. Think about it. All that stuff at the dump just gets thrown away every year"—he nodded at Gunnar—"fifteen hundred pounds of garbage." He gestured back toward the homeless camp. "Meanwhile, these people don't have a shelter over their heads or even enough to eat."

So this all had to do with "freeganism"? Whatever that was, exactly.

"It's a protest?" Min said.

"Sort of. But also…well, kind of a principled stand. I guess you could say we're opting out. We're choosing not to participate in a culture that we think is immoral. Freeganism means we only use exactly what we need in life. We buy as little as possible, mostly living on what we can forage and what other people throw away. That way, we only use exactly what we need."

"Freegansim means we're free!" Venus said, throwing in an annoying little twirl.

Gunnar nodded back at the clearing. "But, I mean, if some people choose not to work, not to earn money, what can you do?"

"Most of the people who are homeless in America are mentally ill," Wade said. "A high percentage are veterans with post-traumatic stress syndrome. There are also a lot of children, or single mothers with children. Even when they do work, they can't afford child care. Sometimes they make it for a while, but then something goes wrong, someone gets sick, and they're out on the streets. It's not that they're lazy like a lot of people think."

Min nodded, her bleeding liberal heart warming to Wade at last. What Wade was saying made sense to me too. Was I being brainwashed by a cult? Was this how it worked? Say things so convincingly that they don't even need to drop a burlap sack over your head?

Wade and Venus would probably say I'd *already* been brainwashed by a cult: the cult of a culture that carelessly wastes so much stuff while other people starve and doesn't even think twice about it. Was that true?

"So you dropped out of school to live in the woods?" I said.

"I finished school," Wade said. "Venus and I both did. And we don't live here in the woods."

"You don't?" I said. "Then where do you live?"

"Not too far. We're squatters." I must've had something of a blank look on my face, because he added, "We live in abandoned houses. It also doesn't seem right to us that some people are homeless when there are all these empty houses around. There's a whole community of us."

I nodded, fascinated—though I wasn't sure if it was the freegans I found interesting or just Wade.

"What do you do for money?" Gunnar said.

"We don't use money, not if we can help it," Wade said. "Like I said, we're opting out." Wade zipped up his backpack. "But Venus and I should go. We're heading the opposite direction you are. You guys know how to get back to your school from here, right?"

"Go?" I said. "Go where?" I was tempted to add, You live in an abandoned house and eat dandelions and Dumpster trash: where exactly would you have to be?

"Oh, we have a whole circuit!" Venus said. "Lots of homeless in this city."

To tell the truth, I was surprised they were leaving. They weren't going to ask us to become freegans? I thought at the very least they were going to ask us for money. Why had they shown us the landfill and the homeless camp anyway? Maybe it was some complicated brainwashing tactic to make us want to learn more about them. If so, it was working.

"See you guys later!" Wade said, even as he disappeared into the trees.

Min and I exchanged a look. This wasn't how she had expected this encounter to end either. Gunnar, meanwhile, was busy typing into his phone.

"Wait!" I said, and Venus stopped and looked back at me. I stared at her stupidly. I didn't know what I wanted to ask her—hell, suddenly I couldn't even remember Wade's name. "Are we ever going to see you again? You and your boyfriend?"

"I'm sure you'll see us around." She started to leave, but then stopped again. "Oh, and Wade and I aren't a couple."

But before I could ask a follow-up question—like did Wade have some *other* girlfriend? Or a boyfriend?—she'd drifted off into the woods too.

Okay, so maybe fate had it out for me after all. I hadn't fallen in love with an ice sculpture exactly, but the same day I'd vowed to forsake love, I'd run into Wade, a homeless, Dumpster-diving freegan.

And I confess: I was smitten.

CHAPTER FOUR

I wanted to talk to someone about my thing for Wade, but I couldn't mention him to Min and Gunnar. Like I said, I hadn't even made it twenty-four hours since I'd forsaken love in front of both of them.

It seemed even weirder to talk to Otto, my new ex, about him. But that night when I was IMing him, Otto surprised me.

OttoManEmpire: So you met someone?

Now this was just uncanny. Otto could still read my mind—even about something like *this*?

Smuggler: WTF?! How did you know?

OttoManEmpire: I didn't! It was a total wild

guess.

Smuggler: I swear to God, it wasn't planned! And it isn't anything yet. I mean, I don't even know if he's gay. I'll probably never even see him again.

OttoManEmpire: Oh, I have a feeling you'll see Wade again.

Wait. I hadn't told Otto Wade's name. So how had Otto known it? Maybe he could read my mind for real! Then I clued in:

Smuggler: You've been following Gunnar's posts. You saw the photos he posted today about Wade and Venus.

OttoManEmpire: LOL. Yeah. Darn, I wanted to make you think I was just brilliant! I figured I could milk this one for weeks.

Smuggler: But I didn't tell Gunnar I thought Wade was hot. Did Gunnar write that?

OttoManEmpire: No. But there's a photo of you staring at him. I could just tell. And, I mean, Wade IS hot.

I smiled. But even so, I wasn't sure what to think about all this. On the other hand, I had wanted someone to talk to about Wade.

Smuggler: Is this weird? You're my ex-boyfriend. It seems like it should be weird talking about this with you.

OttoManEmpire: Yes. No. Maybe. I don't care! I want to know more!

So I told him about Wade, everything Gunnar hadn't already posted, that is.

Smuggler: Have you ever heard of freeganism?

OttoManEmpire: I hadn't, but I looked them up after Gunnar's posts. Part of me doesn't believe it's a real thing.

Smuggler: It's a real thing. And I'm 90% sure he's not a nutcase.

Even as I typed this, I thought: Of course, I'd also been *more* than ninety percent sure that Kevin wasn't hooking up with men in the park at night!

OttoManEmpire: So you're in love with a guy who lives in a Dumpster?

Smuggler: He doesn't LIVE in a Dumpster. That's just where he gets his meals.

I stopped. That didn't sound any better, did it?

Smuggler: And I'm not "in love" with him! I just met him!

OttoManEmpire: I know, I know.

Smuggler: But there is something about him.

How did I explain to him that Wade was exactly the sort of adventure I had been looking for—exactly the kind of thing that had been lacking in my mostly-online relationship with Otto?

Suddenly, I understood exactly why talking to your ex about current boyfriend prospects was a bad idea. Who knew?

OttoManEmpire: Looking for a little walk on the wild side, huh?

Now Otto was back to reading my thoughts, for real this time. This was scary.

Smuggler: Hey, did you ever talk to the guy you were interested in?

OttoManEmpire: No!!!!! He doesn't even know I exist. But you're changing the subject. I wanna hear about your guy!

The truth is there was nothing more to say about Wade. I probably never *would* see him again. And even if I did, just because Wade wasn't with Venus, that didn't mean he was into guys.

The next morning, I found Min in the hallway scraping gum off her locker with a folded three-by-five card.

"Hey," I said.

"How hard is it for people to put their damn gum in a damn trash can?" she said. "Seriously!"

"I know. People at this school are total slobs. You should see the boys' bathroom. There are liquids on the floor in there, I'm not even sure *what* body opening they came out of."

The gum was gooey, and Min's folded card was mostly just spreading it around and making little strands as it stuck to the paper. "Damn it!" she said. "Like I really want to *touch* it when it's been in someone's mouth!"

Gum on your locker is definitely annoying, but Min's reaction seemed a little over-the-top. As chance would have it, I had one of those little disposable toothbrushes in my pocket—I'd started carrying one a couple of months before so I could brush my teeth after lunch. I've also been known to tuck in my shirt and wear clean underwear. What can I say? Sometimes gay stereotypes are true.

I wet the toothbrush with my mouth, then used it on the gum. I kept brushing until it was gone, then wiped the rest away with a Kleenex.

"Thanks," Min said.

I turned to her. "What's wrong?"

"What?" She wouldn't look me in the eye.

"This isn't about gum. Is it Leah?"

Min slumped against her locker. "At the zoo, you were talking about Otto and I was talking about Leah. And here it is, three days later, and you and Otto have broken up."

"What are you saying? You want to break up with Leah?"

"No. But it's like I said before. Something is wrong. Something is *still* wrong. She's keeping secrets."

I was about to tell her I thought she was being ridiculous, that there was no way Leah was keeping secrets from her. But then I remembered Kevin's secrets.

"How about this?" I said. "Why don't we all go out together this weekend? I'll pay special attention to Leah. If she seems weird in any way, we'll figure out what to do next, okay?"

Min considered. "I know you're just humoring me.

47

You think you'll see her, and everything will be totally normal, and you'll be able to use that in order to tell me that I'm wrong, to just move on. But maybe you're right—maybe I *am* imagining things. So I'll give it a try."

I'm embarrassed to admit how much I wanted to see Wade again. But I was pretty sure he didn't have a phone number to call, or even an online profile to stalk. I didn't know his last name anyway.

All I had to go on was the Dumpster where I'd first seen him. So in between classes, I found myself drawn there. If I had even the smallest piece of paper to throw out—the tiniest ball of pocket lint!—I made a point to walk all the way to that stupid, sour-smelling Dumpster.

He wasn't ever there. And did I mention how bad it stank?

I knew returning to the Dumpster was stupid as I was doing it: even if Wade was to come back there again today, he wouldn't do it until the kitchen crew dropped off the trash from lunch. He and Venus had said as much the day before—they had it all timed.

But he wasn't there after school either, even after I watched the kitchen dump its lunch trash. Gunnar and I usually rode home together, but I'd told him to go on without me (I'd lied and said I had to talk to a teacher about a school project).

I lingered by that Dumpster for almost twenty minutes, but Wade never showed. It didn't matter anyway—he probably wasn't even gay. (On the other hand, his clothes had been spotless and, like I said, sometimes gay stereotypes are true!)

I thought: maybe he's in that woods, hanging out at the homeless camp or gathering dandelions and nettles for a wild greens salad.

I didn't have anything better to do, so I decided to check it out. My house was in the opposite direction from the woods, so I decided to leave my bike at the school and come back for it later.

It was a cold winter's day—not freezing, just chilly—and the air under the trees smelled of frost and pine needles. Fortunately, I had on a thick jacket (people who ride their bikes to school every day know how to dress for the weather). It's funny how I hadn't noticed the temperature the day before when I'd been following Wade and Venus.

I walked along the trails. The closest thing to a destination that I had in mind was the homeless camp—that was probably the most likely place for Wade to be. Maybe he brought them food every afternoon, but not necessarily always from the same place. What I hadn't counted on was how confusing those trails were—and I'd been in these woods even before Wade and Venus had taken us here. It was like a maze back there.

I thought I caught a glimpse of something moving

in the trees up ahead. Could it be Wade? But when I tried to follow it, I didn't see anything at all.

Then I saw a flash of blue. This had to be someone's clothing, right? There wasn't anything else in a forest that was blue. Could it be Wade? He hadn't been wearing blue the day before. (I wondered how often he changed his clothes.)

But as quickly as I'd seen it, it was gone. Between the maze of trails and these glimpses through the trees, it felt a little like I was searching for fairies. At least the winter temperature meant I didn't have to worry about being run down by mountain bikers—a real worry in the summer. On the other hand, I *was* all alone back here, except for the people from the homeless camp. And even Wade had said that most homeless people were mentally ill.

I rounded a cluster of bushes and ran right into someone—literally. I'd been so preoccupied looking for glimpses through the trees that I wasn't watching where I was going. We didn't knock heads or fall over, but for a second we stood there, locked together in a tangle of arms, and the other person dropped what they were carrying.

"Sorry!" he said, pulling away. "Sorry about that."

It was Kevin Land.

Yes, *the* Kevin Land. What were the odds? Suddenly, we were two ships crashing in the night. Figures I go looking for Wade and end up with Kevin. Story of my life.

"Kevin," I said. The air was cold, but my voice was colder.

"Russel?" he said. "What are you doing here?" His voice wasn't cold, not at all. Then again, he didn't have any reason to be cold to me, did he?

"I don't know," I said. "I was just out for a walk." Why did I feel guilty? I didn't have anything to feel guilty about. The guy who hooked up with men in the park bushes while waiting for me was the one who had something to feel guilty about!

"Yeah?" he said. "That's great." He bent down to pick up the bag he'd dropped—something from McDonald's. This made sense. There was a McDonald's not too far from the school and this woods, at least as the crow flies. But from the look of the bulging bag, it was a lot of food for one person. Had he picked up food for the whole baseball team? (Kevin was this big baseball player.)

"You heading to practice?" I asked him.

"Practice doesn't start for another week."

"Oh." I should've known this. I'd walked right by the baseball field and there hadn't been anyone on it.

"Coach has us doing some runs on our own. That's why I was back here actually. I've been running here for two weeks now." Sure enough, he was dressed for a run: workout shorts, a sweatshirt, and everything. I noticed something else about him: how handsome he is. That's a cliché, isn't it? To run into an ex-boyfriend and notice how handsome he is? But it was also true.

His chest was thicker even than just the year before, his black hair even more tousled.

"Yeah," I said, "I hear Big Macs are a really good workout."

Kevin stared at me for a second.

"It's a joke," I said, nodding to the bag on the ground. It was a bad joke, but it was still a joke. What the hell was I doing joking around with Kevin anyway?

Kevin sort of shuffled his feet. "Oh. This stuff isn't for me."

"Yeah? Who's it for?"

He thought for a second. "Listen, I should get going. This is getting cold."

"Yeah," I said. He *should* get going. Why was I even talking to him anyway, after the way he treated me?

"See ya around, Russel."

"Yeah," I said.

And he was gone.

After Kevin left, I'm embarrassed to admit I started shaking. I wasn't sure if it was because I was too flushed or too cold. Maybe it was a little of both. Except it probably wasn't either of those things. It was probably just Kevin.

And as I stood there shivering, I realized something. Kevin had said he'd been running in these woods for two weeks now, in preparation for the baseball season. He'd also said that big bag of McDonald's food wasn't for him. If he'd been running in these woods for two weeks, it made sense that he'd have run into the homeless camp eventually. So is that who the hamburgers were for?

Talk about the Elephant of Surprise. Kevin Land, Well-Established Asshole, was delivering meals to the homeless?

CHAPTER FIVE

That Saturday night, I went out to a movie with Min and her girlfriend Leah, just like I'd promised earlier in the week. Gunnar and his girlfriend Em came too.

At first, I was having a good time. The five of us had done stuff as a group before, lots of times. It had never felt like it was two couples and me—like I was a fifth wheel. I mean, I'd had a boyfriend, Otto. He lived in another city, but I'd had him.

But now Otto and I had broken up, and that night as I sat in the theater watching the movie with my friends, it felt totally weird. Isn't that funny? Absolutely nothing was different: it was the same five people, doing basically the same thing we'd always done—even sitting in the same place where we always sat in the theater. But because I no longer had this almost-imaginary, eight-hundred-miles-away boyfriend, I felt like I was all alone.

After the movie, we went to get something to eat on McKenzie Street, which was the one small neighborhood in our town that was even the slightest bit hip and/or trendy. And as we walked down the sidewalk, I was suddenly hyper-aware of how we were arranged—Em and Gunnar walking side-by-side, Min and Leah together, and me.

"Where should we eat?" Em said from up front. She was this sort of bookish type with baggy clothes in earthtone colors and tortoise-shell Harry Potter glasses.

"How about Ethiopian?" Gunnar said. "They have that whole thing where you eat with your hands."

"I don't know," Leah said. "I think I'm sick of Ethiopian." Right then, Min stumbled a little on the sidewalk in front of me. "How about pizza?" Leah said.

"Sounds good to me," Em said.

That decided, we headed toward the restaurant. As we crossed the street, Min drifted back toward me. "Well?" she said.

"Well what?" I said.

"Leah." When I didn't say anything, Min said, "You forgot all about it, didn't you? You said you were going to watch and tell me if she seemed weird!"

"No!" But the truth is I had forgotten. I'd been preoccupied with feeling like a fifth wheel, but I didn't want to admit that to Min. I glanced up at Leah, who is tall and blond and was wearing army fatigues. "I haven't noticed anything yet, but I'll keep looking."

As chance would have it, it was the pizza place where, almost a year earlier, I'd first met up with the other members of the Geography Club, this secret gay alliance I'd been in. I remembered how it had felt so secretive, like we were spies meeting for a rendezvous. If you'd told me then that a year later Min and I would be out and proud, and that I'd have just broken up with my almost-imaginary boyfriend, well, I actually might have believed you.

After we ordered, we sat at the table—me on the end, of course. Then we talked and played tic-tac-toe in the parmesan cheese we'd shaken onto the tabletop. Gunnar, of course, was too busy photographing and posting the conversation to, you know, actually *partici-pate* in any of it.

"How long are you going to keep this up?" I asked him.

"I'm not sure," he said. "I'm pretty sure I'll just know when it's time to quit."

"No one's even following your posts. You know that, right?" Well, no one except Otto, I thought.

"No," he said. "I don't know that."

"Gunnar, I'm your best friend, and last week, *I* unfollowed you."

Everyone laughed at my joke except Gunnar.

"It doesn't matter," he said. "Being followed isn't

the point."

"Then what's the point?"

He thought for a second. "I'm not sure. It's an experiment. Sometimes you don't know the point of an experiment until after it's over. Besides, it's a record of my life. Do people write in a diary because they expect other people to read it? No, just the opposite. They're writing for themselves, to have a record of what they did and thought."

"No one writes in a diary anymore," I said. But even as I said this, I knew Gunnar was making sense.

The pizza took a long time, and I was getting tired of feeling like a fifth wheel, so I volunteered to go see if there was a problem. But on my way to the front counter, I saw Leah slip away to the bathroom. I hadn't really talked to Leah the whole night, not like Min had asked me to, so I stepped over to head her off, to talk to her one-on-one for a minute or two.

But she wasn't going to the bathroom after all. Instead, she ducked into the video game room—currently empty—and pulled out her cell phone. I didn't really think anything about it. So what if she was making a call? She was probably checking in with her mom or maybe a friend from school.

I didn't want to interrupt her phone call, so I started to turn away.

But at the same time, she looked over and saw me.

Right away, she mouthed four words into the phone—I was pretty sure it was "I'll call you later"—and then immediately shut it off. Even now, I wouldn't have thought anything about this except for one thing:

She looked guilty.

She looked like she'd been caught doing something she wasn't supposed to be doing. Was Min right? Was there really something going on with her?

Then she smiled at me—a *big* smile. "Hey!" she said.

"Everything okay?" I said, stepping closer.

"What?" she said. "Oh, yeah! Unquestionably!"

I'm not stupid. I knew she was totally lying.

Later, we went for a walk down McKenzie Street. Em and Leah were now walking together ahead, and Gunnar was busy photographing a fire hydrant (or something), which gave me a chance to pull Min aside.

"Something's going on," I said.

"What?"

"With Leah."

She stared at me. "Are you making fun of me?"

I was a little offended by this: I didn't make fun of my friends! But then I remembered how I'd been totally making fun of Gunnar all dinner long at the pizza place.

"No, I'm serious." I explained how Leah looked suspicious in the video game room. "You need to talk to her."

No one can look at you like you're a total idiot like Min can look at you like you're a total idiot. "Do you really think I haven't tried?" she said. "She's *lying*. That's the whole *point*. No, we need a plan. But we'll have to be discreet."

"Are you serious?"

Min wasn't even listening to me—she was already busy planning Project Expose Leah's Secrets. But I didn't care because it was at that exact moment that I noticed Venus staring at us from across the street. I immediately looked around for Wade too, but she was alone.

I know this sounds like a huge coincidence, our running into her so soon, and maybe it was. On the other hand, Wade and Venus basically lived on the streets—and if there was any street in town where they'd be most welcome, it was here. I wondered how many times I'd walked by them before and just not noticed (or *pretended* not to notice because I didn't want to get involved).

I waved to her. "Venus!" I called to Em and Leah up ahead of us. "Wait up, you guys!"

Venus ran across the street to join us (almost getting hit by a car in the process).

"Russel!" she said. She gave me a big hug, which surprised me even though it shouldn't have. She was wearing the same thing as before—that grimy flight suit—but now she smelled like honey and turpentine.

She felt even skinnier than she looked.

"Hey, Gunnar! Hey, Min!" Venus said, and of course she hugged them too.

"This is Venus," Min said to Leah and Em. "We met her at school earlier this week."

I could tell that Leah and Em were a little surprised that we knew someone who looked like a street bum—or I guess *was* a street bum. Then again, both Leah and Em are really cool, nonjudgmental people. Smiles had already replaced the curiosity on their faces.

"Where's Wade?" I asked Venus. (I couldn't resist.)

"Oh, he's home," she said.

I didn't dare ask her where home was, so instead I said, "So what brings you out here?" But I immediately felt stupid. What did I *think* brought her out there? She was probably looking for dinner.

"Oh, we live around here," Venus said.

Yes! I thought. Needless to say, I really, really wanted to see where they lived—and Wade.

"Oh?" I said, determined to sound casual. "Where's that?"

But before she could answer, Min said to Leah and Em, "Venus is a freegan."

"Vegan?" Em said.

"No, *freegan*," Min said. I was a little afraid that Venus was going to say that we couldn't *tell* them what a freegan is—that we could only *show* them—and I was in no mood to spend an hour walking to the garbage dump and the homeless camp, not with Wade so tantalizingly close by. But Min quickly ran through their world-view—how they'd taken the slogan "reduce, reuse, recycle" to its absolute extreme.

"Wow," Em said. "Interesting."

I focused on Venus again. "So you live around here, huh?"

"Sure do," Venus said. "Wanna see?"

"Sure," I said, still forcing my voice to sound as nonchalant as possible. I turned to the others. "That okay with you guys?"

I don't know what I would've done if someone had said no, but fortunately, everyone else looked almost as curious as I was.

The house was four blocks from the main drag of McKenzie Street, and it looked just like any other house in the neighborhood: an older two-story with a white brick façade and no garage.

Actually, if anything, it looked a little nicer than the other houses on the street. It had been painted recently, and the yard was perfectly maintained—the grass neatly trimmed, the flower beds all weeded.

Venus led us inside where it was a completely different story. The furniture was ratty, the walls were bare, and the carpets were dirty (one of the stains was red, but I was pretty sure it was wine, not blood). There was a dog-eared copy of *Curious George* on the floor and some papers with a cartoon elf on them. It smelled like candle wax and stale sweat.

The house was loud with voices. Six people played cards around a coffee table: four guys and two girls. They basically ignored us, but I noticed that except for one guy in his forties, they were all college-age-ish. They were also all pretty scruffy (and the guys all had beards), but they didn't seem unhealthy—except for one girl, who looked sort of anemic, pale and frail. Unlike Wade, their clothes were all pretty tattered and dirty. The anemic girl had sewn together a rip in her pants with what looked like dental floss.

Gunnar, of course, took photos of it all for his online profile.

"Hey, I know you guys!" said a voice from the kitchen. Wade stepped into sight. "Min! And Gunnar? And Russel." I couldn't help but notice that he'd acknowledged me last, and he didn't hug us the way Venus had. Then again, maybe he didn't want to come across as too forward.

Wait. Ignore all that. These contradictory thoughts of mine will drive you crazy if you let them. God knows, they drive me crazy.

I will say this: Wade's white t-shirt was spotless again. I know I was totally relying on stereotypes, but at this point it was all I had. That t-shirt was also *tight*, which means I had a better look at his body. It was a mountain I definitely wanted to climb.

"So," I said, still determined to sound casual. "This is your house."

"Well, it's not 'our' house," Wade said. "We don't really believe in personal possessions. But it's the house where we live."

"How exactly do you manage that?" Min said. To her credit, there was still no judgment in her voice.

"It started out as a foreclosure," Wade said. "It hadn't been occupied for at least a year. When we first moved in, the neighbors were really happy to see us. They thought someone had finally bought the house. That's the thing about property. Who's to say who really owns what? How do I know you didn't rip off that jacket? We all just sort of take each other's word.

"Then word got out that we didn't own the house and weren't paying rent to the bank, and it got a little ugly. But freegans aren't really the same thing as squatters. It's a movement for us, right? It's not just us being lazy or angry at the world. So we understand you can't just piss people off and expect to get anywhere. That's why we take care of the places where we live. We're all in this together—in our communities and on this planet. That's the freegan motto. Once the neighbors realized a house with a bunch of freegans is a lot better than a house with a bunch of squatters, or even just an abandoned house, things got better."

As Wade was talking, I couldn't help but think: if this had been any neighborhood other than the one it was, the neighbors would have been on them with torches and pitchforks, no matter that they painted the house or mowed the lawn. But attitudes were a little looser in this neck of the woods. Even so, I definitely saw the strategy of keeping the yard so spotless. Why ask for trouble?

"You really *live* here?" Em said. "And no one works?"

"Oh, *everyone* works," Wade said. "We're not free-loaders. If you don't work, you can't stay. Same if you're an addict. You can't stay here if you're using. We're really firm about that."

Wade gestured to a bulletin board in the hallway into the kitchen. Every square inch was covered with snapshots. "These are all the people who've visited us in the last year," he said.

I scanned the photos even as Gunnar took a picture of the pictures. Once again, most of the faces were young and scruffy—and almost every white person had a deep tan. I also noticed that someone had rested a small monkey wrench on the top of the bulletin board's wood frame.

"Here you go!" Venus said, turning around from the kitchen counter and handing me a glass of something that looked like cider.

"What is it?"

"Dandelion wine! Don't you remember? I promised I'd give you some!"

I smiled, but I didn't say that what she'd promised was to make me a wild greens salad with nettles.

I took a sip.

"It's good," I said, and I wasn't lying. I'd had wine

once before, but this tasted sweeter and more earthy—like liquid corn on the cob, if that makes any sense.

"How do you pay the bills?" Min asked. "Water and electricity?" It was only when she said this that I realized, yes, the house definitely had utilities—the lights were on and everything. It's funny how you take stuff like that so much for granted that it's almost invisible.

"They make us pay in advance," Wade said. "Cashier's check. But we get by. Some of us do temp work—yard work or construction. Others sell crafts. And we sometimes get donations. I'd love for us to live without any money whatsoever, but that's pretty much impossible in the modern world. The only rule is that everyone contributes."

"What do you do for clothing?" Em asked.

"We share!" Venus said.

"Well, not exactly," Wade said. "Come on, I'll show you." He led us to the back door, then out into the small backyard and through the darkness, toward a freestanding garage along a gravel alley.

The door to the garage was unlocked. When Wade turned on the light inside, there was no car, just tables and bins of old clothing: shirts and shoes and pants and belts. Another table held toiletries—toothpaste and toothbrushes, tampons, dental floss, toilet paper. Built-in shelves lined the back wall, and they were crammed with camping supplies—lanterns, rolled-up blankets, and candles—but also the kinds of things you'd expect to find in a garage: cans of spray paint, a crate of what looked like fireworks, and all kinds of different tools, from pliers to clippers. The air smelled like motor oil and something chalky.

I touched an itchy wool sweater on a table. "What is all this?" I said.

"The freegan store," Wade said.

"Store? I thought you didn't use money."

"We don't. It's not like other stores. Everything here is free. Take what you need. You just have to be sure to leave something for someone else. We're all in this together, remember?" He pointed to a stack of long-sleeved, button-down shirts, still in their plastic packages. "I found these in a Dumpster out at the mall."

Needless to say, Gunnar took pictures of it all.

Em picked up a pair of gloves made out of red yarn.

"Amy made those—this girl who lived here just before Christmas," Venus said. "She knitted them herself."

Em thought for a second, then unwound the scarf she was wearing. She folded it up and put it on one of the tables. Then she put the gloves on.

"That's it!" Wade said, a big smile on his face. "That's exactly right."

Meanwhile, I was kicking myself. If I'd thought of it first, I could have impressed Wade by trading something too—the plastic comb in my pocket for a pencil.

Or maybe I could do something really dramatic and generous: my jacket for a couple of pairs of socks?

Was it too late to do it now? Maybe I could start this whole chain of events with each one of us dramatically trading something we owned for something else. Well, technically Em would have started it, but still. It could be a whole "thing." That would impress Wade, right? Or would it just look phony and desperate for attention?

"You know," Leah said, nodding to her cell phone, "I should probably go."

"Yeah?" Min said.

I didn't want to leave yet. I'd managed to find Wade again, but I hadn't really gotten his attention. I didn't want to go without making some kind of connection.

Leah looked at me—she probably saw the annoyance in my eyes. "But you guys don't have to leave—you can stay."

Before I could say anything, Em said, "No, no, you're right. We should all probably get going."

So that was it. We'd come in two cars: Min's and Em's. If they both wanted to leave, I had to go. I thought about asking Wade for his phone number or his email address, but then I remembered he didn't have a phone or a computer. And I didn't want to say anything in front of Min or Gunnar that made it too obvious I was into Wade, not after forsaking love earlier that week. Besides, it would've sounded stupid—I barely knew him. I knew where he lived now, but it's not like I had any excuse to come back, at least not without looking like a total dork.

He walked us to the front door and then he said, "Well, I guess I'll see you around." Once again, he was talking to the group, not to me in particular.

"Yeah," I said. "See you." But even as I said it, I wondered if I ever would.

CHAPTER SIX

I didn't get a chance to go into any detail with Min about Leah until the next day, Sunday. It was early afternoon when she joined Gunnar and me in my bedroom.

"Tell me exactly what you saw," Min said. "Don't leave anything out." It was the first thing she said when she entered. I was sitting on the bed, and Gunnar was working on my computer. For what it's worth, my bedroom includes everything from my middle school swimming trophies to my collection of plastic collectibles from animated Disney movies. (What can I say? I'm a bewitching mix of contradictions!) On the nightstand, my lava lamp oozed.

"Well, maybe it wasn't anything," I told Min. I went through what I'd seen step-by-step. I admitted the only real evidence I had was that she'd looked guilty.

"Guilty of what?" Min said.

"I don't know. Just guilty."

"See? I told you! She's hiding something!"

"Min."

"What?"

"You know what. You need to talk to her. You need to ask her what's going on."

Min was back to looking at me like I was a total idiot. "I already told you. I can't talk to her. But I have a plan. She and her whole family are out of town next weekend."

I laughed. "So what, you're going to break into her house and check out her bedroom?"

"Yes. Well, *we* are."

I gaped. I'm not sure I've ever gaped before in my life, but I did it now. "*Min!* I was *joking!*"

"What? It's the only way to really know what's going on."

"Well, that and actually, you know, *talking* to her."

"I already told you—"

"Yeah, yeah, she's lying, so you can't talk to her. Can we just think about this for one second?"

"I *have* thought about it. I'm going *crazy* thinking about it. Now I need some action." She sat down next to me on the bed. To her credit, she finally realized I was looking at her like *she* was the idiot. "What?"

"You know what," I said. "This is going to lead to total disaster. You, Gunnar, and I break into Leah's house because you're worried about her breaking up with you, but the fact that we break into her house is exactly the thing that makes her break up with you. It's an ironic paradox, like in an old episode of *Star Trek*."

Gunnar hadn't said a word since Min arrived, hadn't even looked over at us at my mention of his name, at my casual inclusion of him in Min's crazy plan—he'd been too busy on the computer. But at my mention of *Star Trek*, he immediately perked up.

"Talk about tempting fate!" I went on, still talking to Min.

"Maybe I was totally wrong about this, but I was under the impression the three of us were friends," Min said.

"Min—"

"Really *good* friends," she said. "*Best* friends. And that part of being best friends is that we can all count on each other. We're the voice at the end of each other's bat-phones. Well, right now I need help, so I'm sending up the bat-signal."

At the mention of Batman, Gunnar looked over at us again. Min was really playing hardball here.

"Part of friendship is also calling people on their shit," I said.

Min nodded. "And you did, and I appreciate it. I totally acknowledge your very appropriate shit-calling. But in full knowledge of the shit that's been called, I still want to move forward on this. So the question becomes: are you in or are you out?"

I looked at Gunnar, and he looked at me. Finally, he nodded. Min hadn't just played the "friend" card— she'd dressed it up in all kinds of cool Batman imagery. Gunnar and I were powerless to resist.

Min wanted to go plan the break-in, but before she did, she stopped at Gunnar sitting at the computer.

"Don't post one word about this online," she said. "Are we clear?"

He nodded stiffly, and then she was gone.

Gunnar kept typing away on my computer, which was actually fine with me. It gave me a chance to do some thinking—not about Wade, who was probably out of my life forever. All this talk about Leah had me thinking about Kevin again. (Was it possible that I could spend even a single day not obsessing about a guy? No, so stop asking.)

I sat back on my bed.

How was it I was pretty sure I'd seen Kevin delivering food to that homeless camp? If Kevin was the jerk I thought he was, why would he be doing that? Yeah, yeah, people are complicated, blah, blah, blah. But let's face it: people aren't *that* complicated. Most of the time, cool people are cool, and assholes are, well, assholes. Sure, assholes will be cool when it helps them in some way, when it involves something important to *them*. But isn't that the very definition of an asshole? That they only care about something when it *is* important to them? It's when you don't get anything out of it and you still do the right thing, that's what makes a person cool. *By definition.*

And once an asshole, always an asshole. Right? Tigers don't change their stripes, and you can't teach an old dog new tricks. People don't change.

So what the hell was Kevin doing delivering food to the homeless? Was it possible he wasn't the person I thought he was? But I'd *seen* him hooking up with a guy while he was waiting for me at that park! With my own eyes! And when I'd confronted him, he'd basically been a total prick about it, telling me to get lost.

I sat upright on my bed. "What do you think of Kevin?" I asked Gunnar.

He thought for a second, but kept typing. "Cannot predict now."

"What?" I said, confused. Did he not want to be distracted from updating his profile?

"Better not tell you now."

"Gunnar, you're not making any sense."

"Reply hazy, try again."

Finally, I clued in. Gunnar was ironically quoting the Magic 8-Ball. Or maybe it wasn't so ironic. The truth is he was reciting only the vague or non-committal answers.

"Wait," I said. "So you don't have any opinion?"

"Difficult to see," he said. "Always in motion is the future." Now he was quoting Yoda from *Star Wars*, but the principle was the same.

On one hand, I was vaguely annoyed by Gunnar's non-answers. On the other hand, the fact that he didn't have a clear opinion was sort of an answer in itself. What Gunnar was saying was that even he—who, like I said, often surprised me by picking up on things other people didn't notice—couldn't quite get a handle on Kevin.

Why did that excite me exactly?

"Can I talk to you for a second?" I said.

"Sure." Gunnar spun away from the computer, giving me his full attention at last. I explained everything that had happened with Kevin. He'd already known about the incident in the park last fall, so I told him about my running into Kevin in the woods.

When I was done, Gunnar said, "Why do you care?"

"Huh?"

"Why all the sudden interest in Kevin? Are you saying you wanna get back together with him?"

Was that what I was saying? Was that what all this thinking and talking was really all about?

"I guess I hadn't really thought that far ahead," I said, and it was the truth. But Gunnar's question did make sense. I mean, Kevin was the first guy I'd ever loved—in more ways than one (yes, I'm talking about sex). Why would I care if he was a decent person if I wasn't interested in maybe dating him again? I already had plenty of friends.

I shifted, and the bed squeaked. "I know what

you're thinking."

"What am I thinking?"

"You're thinking I'm an idiot—that only last week I was saying I'd completely forsaken love."

"No, I was thinking about this new video editing program I was reading about last night."

Was Gunnar joking with me? He looked completely serious, but with Gunnar, you can never really tell.

"What do you wanna do?" he said.

"I guess I want to find out what kind of person Kevin really is," I said. "Do some research."

"You mean spy on him like what Min wants to do with Leah?"

"No! This is totally different!"

"It doesn't seem very different."

"Well, it is! For one thing, Leah is Min's actual girl-friend, someone who's supposed to tell her the truth. Kevin is someone who did some pretty bad things before, so I want to know more about him before I consider dating him again."

Gunnar just kept staring at me. The truth is I'd been waiting until after Min left to bring this up. I hadn't really thought about it at the time, but didn't that prove I was worried about being a hypocrite—that some unconscious part of me realized Min would make the obvious connection?

"Okay, okay!" I said. "I'm a hypocrite. But now I'm the one sending up the 'friend' bat-signal. Are you going to help me or not?"

There was never a question in my mind that he would.

The first thing I decided to do was just sort of keep an eye on Kevin at school. It's funny because I'd been doing this all along, but I'd always felt bad for doing it, so I'd tried to pretend I *wasn't* doing it, even to myself. It's a little like how I'd spent my entire life feeling bad about checking out hot guys in general. I did it, but I didn't want people to know I did it, and I even kind of wanted to pretend to myself I didn't do it. It's one thing for a guy to check out a hot girl, which happens *constantly*. Straight guys are completely open about it—too open about it, actually. It's basically, like, sexual harassment, the comments and calls that straight guys make in our school hallways every second of every day. But a gay guy checking out another guy, especially a straight guy? That's something entirely different, at least for some straight guys. They don't want any indication at all, ever, that some guy is thinking of them in a sexual way.

Basically, straight guys don't want to be treated by gay guys the way they've been treating girls their whole lives. Which is just crazy unfair. And even without thinking about it, I'd been totally buying into it. It was making me angry now that I thought about it, which I never really had before.

The point is—yes, I got a little off-topic there—I

watched Kevin from a distance. And by the middle of the week, I had learned a few new things about him.

The biggest thing I noticed was that he didn't have a whole lot of friends. He'd used to be one of the most popular kids in school, but he wasn't now.

Kevin did have one friend—Ben, one of his buddies from the baseball team. At first I wondered if they were boyfriends, but it was pretty clear they weren't. I'm not sure how I could tell—I mean, it's not like they'd be holding hands in the hallway, not in our school. But they also weren't going to great lengths to *not* touch either, you know? Does that make sense?

I also never once saw Kevin bully or tease anyone else, even in a light-hearted way. Was this because he'd come out as gay, so he was more sensitive to others now? Or maybe his coming out had knocked him far enough down the popularity ladder that no one took him seriously as a bully anymore. (There was a depressing thought buried in there somewhere: on some level, did you need to be a bully to be popular? The whole "alpha" thing?)

Then on Wednesday afternoon on my way out of school, I happened to pass by the library, and I caught a glimpse of Kevin and a friend sitting at a table near the door. They were laughing, and it was such a warm, easy snicker between the two of them I might have stopped to listen even if it hadn't been Kevin. I knew immediately it was like that moment I'd shared with Min the week before—where you're not just in the same instant in time, you're sharing the same emotion.

Was this Kevin's new boyfriend? I admit I wanted to know that too.

No. I knew the guy Kevin was sitting with, and he was straight.

It was Brian Bund. He's a really good guy, but he's also someone who was the unquestioned outcast of the whole school, the lowest of the low. He had acne, a stutter, the whole bit.

I wasn't sure I'd ever even seen Brian laugh before. That's why I hadn't recognized him at first—he looked completely different now. His face was so much brighter, more open, with a big scythe of a smile, cutting me right down to size. Brian and I were still friends—he was straight, but he came to the school's GSA meetings, and I almost always said hi to him when I saw him in the hallway. But I guess I can't say we'd become friend-friends.

But Kevin and Brian had?

As I watched them, I realized Kevin looked different now too. That impish, smirk-y, somewhat cocky face that I'd fallen so madly in love with? It was deeper, more serious, or maybe more real, like Pinocchio becoming an actual little boy (I warned you I like animated Disney movies). Even his laugh seemed richer now.

Kevin caught me looking at him. The laughter froze on his face even as I immediately turned away.

It was funny how I'd been watching Kevin all

these months out of the corner of my eye, but there were all these things I'd missed, obvious things that I should have seen. I'd been sneaking peeks at him, checking out the hang of his sweatshirt (or the bulge of his ass), but I guess I'd never really looked at *him*, not until just this week.

Gunnar had a dentist's appointment after school, so I headed for my bike alone, but I couldn't stop thinking about Kevin.

None of this made sense. Kevin had been a total jerk to me in the park that night. And yet now here he was going around the school looking all real and serious, even as he laughed in the library with Brian Bund. This wasn't the Elephant of Surprise—it was the Elephant of Fuck With Your Mind.

As I passed by the Dumpster, a head poked up.

"Wade?" I said.

"Russel!" he said with a smile. "I was hoping I'd run into you."

CHAPTER SEVEN

Wade was hoping he'd run into me?

"Really?" I said. "Me?" It was a little like one of those moments in movies where the loser main character is glancing around to make sure he's really the person being spoken to. I stopped thinking about Kevin, that's for sure.

"Really," he said. He climbed out of the Dumpster (the muscles in his arms really bulged). "I got a good vibe from you the other day. You seem like a decent person."

I blushed. I mean, he was flirting with me, right?

I nodded to his backpack, which didn't look particularly full. "So how was the haul?"

"Not so good. I should've known. Wednesdays always suck. Mondays, Thursdays, and Fridays are the best days, at least at schools and hospitals." When I stared at him for an explanation, he added, "Cafeteria food deliveries are usually Mondays and Thursdays, so that's when kitchens need to make room in their cupboards and refrigerators. And Fridays are the days they throw out all the stuff they think will spoil over the weekend."

"Ah," I said. "So why come today?"

He fiddled with the straps on his backpack. "Well, like I said, I was hoping I'd run into you."

Wade had been looking for me exactly the same way I'd been looking for him? This did nothing to stop my blushing. There was no possible way I was misinterpreting all this, was there? Validate my reality here.

"So nothing for the homeless camp?" I said.

"Not today. But they'll get by." Especially if Kevin was running fast food over their way, I thought. Who knows? Maybe the whole city was secretly feeding that homeless camp, like the stray cat who goes from house to house and ends up the best fed animal in the whole neighborhood. But I didn't mention that to Wade, because I suspected he wouldn't appreciate the analogy.

"Can I ask you a question?" I said.

"Sure," he said.

"How old are you?"

"Nineteen."

I nodded. That looked about right.

"So…" I said.

He laughed. "How did I end up like this? A freegan?"

"Well, kinda."

He thought for a second. "That's not something I can tell you. It's something I can only *show* you."

I rolled my eyes. "I totally should've seen that coming, shouldn't I?"

He beamed. "Yup! So? You got some time?"

"You mean like right now? Without Min and Gunnar?"

"They can come too. If you really want."

If you really want. That's what he'd said. But what he'd meant was that he wanted to spend time with me. Alone. He was totally hitting on me! Right? I mean, this wasn't all in my mind. *Please* validate my reality here!

"Sure," I said. "I guess. But, I mean, I still have my bike."

"I came on a bike too. I borrowed it from the freegan house. Which is good because where we're going to is too far to walk."

Wade's freegan bike was surprisingly pathetic—a bent and squeaky thing with brake levers that were attached to the handlebars with actual twist-ties. It was a nice reminder that as romantic as freeganism seemed in theory, the reality of it was pretty different.

Wade led me to a nearby residential neighborhood. The houses were all small and old—mostly one-story with chain-link fences and lawns where the dandelions were the only things still alive. I could smell the exhaust and burnt rubber from the freeway a couple of streets over.

Wade stopped his bike in front of one particular house. It looked pretty much like all the others, except it had a weathered white picket fence, not a chain-link one. And off to one side was a mangled trike that looked like it had been run over by a car.

"This is where I grew up," he said, simply enough.

I glanced back the way we'd come. "Wait. Did you go to Goodkind?" This was my high school, only a couple of miles away.

He nodded. Somewhere in the distance, some asshole wouldn't stop revving his motorbike.

I thought back. "You were a senior when I was a freshman!"

"Yup."

Why hadn't I recognized him before? Because I hadn't expected to find a graduate from our school rummaging around in the Dumpster? But it was also that he looked so different: he'd been bookish and quiet and lanky then, and didn't have a shaved head. Now he was a lot more filled out (how he'd gained weight as a freegan, I didn't know).

But it wasn't just that. I remembered him looking sort of shell-shocked, which isn't something a freshman usually thinks about a senior. Now he wasn't like that at all: he seemed bold, confident, a natural born leader—a different person completely.

"You're probably thinking I had this terrible childhood," Wade said. "That my parents divorced, that I grew up miserable, and now I've rejected the whole middle class lifestyle."

"No!" I said, except that's pretty much exactly what I'd been thinking.

"Well, it's sort of true. I mean, my early childhood was great. My parents were great. I was an only kid, but I was a good student, so they had big plans for me—my whole family did, my grandparents, my aunts and uncles. I was going to be the first member of my family to go to college. I was going to be the one to change the world. It was all going according to plan, but then when I was about twelve, my dad got sick. A year later, he died."

"Wow, that sucks," I said.

"My mom took it hard. But it didn't change anything. She was determined to keep the house, even if it meant her working two jobs. Which it did. But everything was different. Before, the future—my future—had been this happy, joyful thing, like we were all on this road trip to California. Now it was the exact opposite of joy. Now it was something I absolutely *had* to do, the only thing that would make my mom and my dead dad's whole lives worthwhile. It started to feel like I was heading somewhere completely out of my control, like I was marching off to some kind of prison camp. But of course, I couldn't tell my mom any of this."

I nodded. My childhood had been totally different than Wade's, but I understood where he was coming from. Especially the part about not being able to tell your parents what you really feel.

Without another word, he started forward on the bike again. I guess that meant we weren't going inside. For all I knew, his mother didn't even live there anymore. Even if she did, how likely was it that she'd accepted her freegan son? From a parent's point of view, that had to be even worse than being gay. (And what if he was freegan *and* gay, which is what I desperately hoped?)

As we headed down the street, we passed a woman in an orange waitress' uniform scraping dog shit off her shoe in the gravel next to her driveway. At first, she just scowled at us, but Wade waved, and she recognized him and smiled, rolling her eyes at her messy shoe. I wondered if she knew he was a freegan now.

He led me down a couple more streets, then into a vacant lot and up a trail to a grassy hill where we could look out over the city on the other side, and I couldn't help but think of that Charles Dickens story *A Christmas Carol,* where the ghosts take Ebenezer Scrooge on a tour of his life, except that rather than show me my life, Wade was showing me his.

Wade pointed to the building right below—it was white and boxy like a hospital. "That's where my mom worked the night shift. It's a nursing home. It's also where she lost it one night."

"Lost it?"

"She cut the cords to all the call-buttons. Basically, she snapped. So she got 'sent away' for a while."

"Sent away?"

"A mental hospital."

"Ah," I said. "How old were you?"

"Seventeen. It was halfway through my senior year."

Talk about shell-shocked, I thought.

"Some relatives pitched in, and the plan was for me to stay in the house by myself until my mom got better, or until it was time for me to go away for college."

"Yeah? So?"

He pointed again, to a building down the road beyond the hospital—a supermarket. "I had a job—I'd had a job all through school. First, I was a bag boy, but I worked my way up to checker. That's where I met my first freegan. For a long time, I'd been surprised by how much food we threw out—even after the food banks came and took all the expired food they could. Then I noticed these people who would gather around the Dumpsters. It wasn't easy to get inside—supermarkets have Dumpsters that lock for a reason. But I got to know them. Eventually I started 'accidentally' leaving it unlocked. And I got to talking to them. I liked them. It wasn't too long after that we lost the house."

"So you were homeless?"

"Not really. I mean, I could've stayed with relatives. Or I could've left for college three months early and stayed on the campus. But something just hit me: I didn't need a job if I didn't have a place to stay. If I joined the freegans, I could take the summer off, and then go to college in the fall."

"And so you did."

"And so I did."

"What did you think?"

It was like his eyes reached out and grabbed me by the shoulders. "It was amazing! Living with the freegans was the exact opposite of the last five years of my life. I didn't have to be anywhere I didn't want to be or do anything I didn't want to do. For the first time since I could remember, my life wasn't just about doing what other people wanted me to do, what other people *expected* of me. I was free!"

That's just what Venus had said: freeganism meant being free. But then I thought: free to eat out of Dumpsters and drive a bike held together with twist-ties?

He must've seen what I was thinking on my face, because he said, "I know how it sounds. It's so hard to explain. Remember, I used to live like everyone else, like you do. I know what it's like to live in both worlds. But most people don't know what it's like to live like a freegan, not wanting things, not worrying about the future."

"Not worrying about the future?" How could this

be? Wouldn't you *always* be worrying about the future—about your next meal, or what happens when your one pair of shoes wears out?

"That's just it," Wade said. "The world provides. It always does. You don't always get what you want, but you always get what you need. It takes an attitude adjustment. But once you make it, you don't have to spend all your time thinking about the future, wanting and planning. You can just live in the moment. Can you imagine that? Being totally satisfied with your life exactly the way it is?"

"I guess," I said. "And suddenly it's not your responsibility to change the world."

"But that's just it! Before, everyone *expected* me to change the world, but I never knew what that meant. Now I do. It's not until you stop worrying about your own selfish wants and needs that you become aware— *really* aware—of what's going on around you. How do archeologists study a culture? They look at the trash, at the stuff that got left behind, right? Well, that's what we freegans do too! We see things the way they really are, the secrets people keep. When you live the way we do, when you don't spend your whole life looking at a television or a computer screen, you can't help but take a good long look at the world. And you see things, things that were hidden before, people that are forgotten or ignored. A lot of people want you to go on ignoring these things and these people, but you can't. Once you really *see* them, once you see that they're people just like you, you can't not see them again. So when it comes to changing the world, I feel like now I know exactly what needs to change. And I *want* to change it—not because someone thinks I should, but because *I* want to. And I think I *am* changing the world. It's not like I dropped out of life by becoming a freegan. I still live in the world. I just see it with different eyes. It's this weird paradox. By giving up all the things I thought were so important, I care a lot more about life and about the world. I realized I didn't need to go to college to change it! And I *will* change it. I'll do what I have to do to change the world. Whatever it takes—anything at all."

Wade's enthusiasm was infectious. It was impossible not to smile. I was sure that the odds of my ever becoming a freegan were about the same as my dating girls again, but I had to admit it was an interesting point of view—definitely one I hadn't ever heard before.

"Some freegans think we should drop out," Wade went on. "That we *have* dropped out—that we should reject everyone and everything else. But that's not how I see it. We *are* a part of society—why should we be considered any less American than anyone else? We just see things differently. And I think we can see the future. There's a revolution coming, Russel. You can feel it in the trees—you can taste it in the dandelions. Like I said, you might not see it if you spend all day staring at a computer screen. But it's definitely coming!"

On one hand, this whole Passionate and Idealistic Young Man thing was totally working for me. On the other hand, even I'm not this wild-eyed.

"A revolution?" I said. Of people eating out of Dumpsters? For me, that's what it kept coming back to. I'm sure Wade could hear the skepticism in my voice.

"The world can't go on the way it is. It just can't! Why should this small percentage of people consume more and more while everyone else just gets less and less? The planet won't allow it. Why should everyone else? Why *would* everyone else?"

"Well, yeah, but…"

"What?"

A wind blew, kicking up dust on the top of that hill. I shook my head. "Nothing. Forget it."

"No. I want to hear what you have to say."

"Well, okay, let's say you're totally right about limited resources, and the dying planet, and the crazy distribution of wealth, and all the rest. I actually agree with you about all that."

He smiled, enjoying this. "Okay, yeah."

"Well, how are you changing any of that? You're consuming less, and that's great. But how many of you are there? Ten? Out of a city of hundreds of thousands? You're not changing anyone's mind. You're doing all this stuff, but people don't even know you're doing it."

"They can see," Wade said. "People know we're here."

I shook my head. "They don't. You've become the person you used to ignore. If people notice you at all, it's to laugh at you or pity you or judge you." I hesitated, not wanting to hurt his feelings. Then again, he'd said he wanted to hear. "This is the Internet era. You can complain about computer or TV screens all you want, but that's where people live, especially young people, the people you need to persuade if you really want to change the world. Maybe you're listening to the trees, but those people aren't. They're listening to their iPods."

"Without trees, there are no iPods!"

"Eventually, I guess," I said. "But in the meantime, people don't care. Your ideas are great—they're really, really cool. And maybe you do know people better than any of us—maybe you *do* know all our secrets or hidden things. But what difference does it make if people have never heard of you?"

"You think we're irrelevant?"

I actually laughed. "Are you kidding? This is America, land of mini-vans and shopping malls. And you're telling people not to own things? Of course you're irrelevant! Completely and totally irrelevant! But that's not even the point."

"What's the point?" he said. Wade had a little of that shell-shocked expression I remembered from when we'd gone to the same high school. But I couldn't stop now.

"You're missing an opportunity," I said.

"How?"

"People are connected now, in a way they've never been connected in all of human history—thanks to technology, I mean. In some ways, that's probably bad. I know all the arguments: we're not connecting to each other as human beings anymore—we're only connecting as blips on a screen, as images, as ideas. But in some ways, it's really good."

"How is it good?" Wade asked.

"Well, for one thing, it means that things can change a lot faster than ever before. It doesn't take years or months or weeks for a new idea to travel around the whole country or even the whole world. It can happen in a matter of hours. Minutes!" I should admit that by this point, I was totally quoting from my Media Studies teacher. But it sounded good, right?

"Freegans are online," Wade said. "We have a website."

"That's a start. But it's not the same thing—that's not what I'm talking about. You have to meet people where they are. You have to speak their language. Would you listen to someone who had never lived like a freegan, who didn't know anything about you, who came up to you and started offering you advice?"

"If it made sense, I might."

"Even if they were telling you to stop doing everything you're doing, everything you love?"

Wade fell silent, and I was just hoping I hadn't hurt his feelings. Finally, he nodded. "I hear what you're saying. You can't change things from the outside. That's what a lot of freegans say. They're freegans for themselves. They don't care about changing the world."

"If you want to change things, you can be a little outside the world. Hell, maybe you *have* to be outside some. But not as far out as you are."

He thought for a second, then grinned. "So maybe that's why I met you."

"Me?" This wasn't what I'd expected him to say.

He lifted an eyebrow. "Sure. Now that you've met freegans, you can tell others. Or write about us online."

"Oh, I'm no great communicator. If you want someone to help you get your message out online, you should talk to Gunnar."

His eyes gripped me again. "You're wrong, Russel. You're really smart. And you're a really good guy."

I blushed. Now he was back to flirting with me again, right? I mean, there wasn't any question, was there? I ask again: validate my feelings, please!

"What does your mom think about all this?" I was no fool. I knew when it was time to change the subject.

Wade deflated like a balloon. I'd asked exactly the wrong question.

"I haven't really told her," he said. "I mean, I've

tried to tell my whole family. I know they suspect I live on the street. But I guess I've never actually said the word 'freegan.' I know they wouldn't understand. My mom is barely talking to me. And everyone else, they're just totally pissed that I didn't go to college, like I've betrayed some sacred trust, like I've betrayed my dad, by doing what I want to do rather than what they want me to do. Either that or they pity me, like my mind snapped like my mom's, just at a younger age."

"That sucks," I said. What else could I say? My heart totally bled for Wade. When I'd come out as gay to my parents, it had been a huge deal. But they'd gotten over it after a while. Sort of.

He shrugged it off. "It doesn't matter. We'll all probably be moving on soon anyway."

"Who?"

"The whole house. The plan is to move to the big city—there's an even bigger freegan community there. The freegans are my only family now."

Leaving town? But I'd only just met him.

"Still…" he said, looking down. It was like he was trying to make a decision about something.

"What?"

"Can I show you one other thing?" he said, almost a whisper. "This is probably the most important thing of all."

"Sure," I said. I had no idea what it was, but I hope I don't have to tell you I was *dying* to see it.

* * *

Back on our bikes, we headed off again, down the hill, and under the freeway and into a valley that led straight to the downtown area. It was late afternoon by now, and we'd left the residential area behind. The whole valley had once been the industrial part of town, but most of the businesses had long since moved on, leaving crumbling brick warehouses with broken windows and fading painted names on the sides—names like Beacon Industrial and Comstock Shoe Company. A rail line had once run through the valley too, but it had long been abandoned, and the tracks that remained were mostly covered with weeds. But there were still a few businesses left, like a pickle plant where they marinated the cucumbers in these giant round tubs that were almost as big as water towers. You could smell the dill and brine for blocks around. Meanwhile, the side roads were so old that some of them were still paved with red bricks and cobblestones. Between the bricks and the railroad tracks, it made for lousy biking. But before too long, Wade pulled his bike into the gravel lot next to an old wooden warehouse. It had the same square shape as all the other old warehouses in the area, but it reminded me of an old barn—I guess because it was wood and the planks seemed warped and creaky, like the whole structure might collapse at any moment.

"What's this?" I said.

"It's cool. It's abandoned." For a freegan, I guess that was a good thing.

We pulled our bikes into a little patch of trees alongside the building. There was a rusted metal door in front of the building—at least the size of a garage door—but it was sealed tight, so Wade led me around the side of the building. I knew I should have been more wary. I mean, it's never a good idea to break into abandoned buildings, especially ones that look like they might collapse at any moment. But I wasn't worried about being kidnapped by a cult anymore—or maybe I was just so deep into the brainwashing that I couldn't even see it for the brainwashing it was. Something about Wade told me that he was on the level, that I could trust him. Or maybe it was as simple as I just wanted get on with that adventure I said I'd been so eager to have.

At the far edge of the building, there was another smaller door, located along the ground. It must have been for some kind of vent, but it had been boarded up too, with darkened two-by-fours.

Wade crouched down and started pulling out the bottom two-by-fours. I guess they hadn't been nailed in place, or if they had been, someone had already pulled them free.

In a minute, there was a gap that was just big enough for a person, at least if you crawled in on your stomach.

Which is exactly what Wade did. I watched him

squirm his way in until his worn tennis shoes disappeared all the way into the warehouse.

I followed behind.

It was dark, but not as dark as it could've been. There was a row of windows up along the ceiling—windows that had mostly long since been broken, something that explained the thick layer of dried pigeon poop along the floor. Or maybe it was bat guano, which was disturbing considering I'd just put my hands in it. As my eyes adjusted to the dark, I also saw a layer of trash covering the floor: loose sheets of plastic and opened tin cans. A rusted metal barrel sat off to one side. The cavernous roof was held up by thick wooden pillars. The whole area smelled of dirt and must, but even in here, I could still smell the brine from that nearby pickle factory.

It was mostly empty, except for a glass-walled office in the corner across from us.

I looked at Wade. He surprised me by turning and putting the two-by-fours back in place.

"So no one sees we're inside," he said by way of explanation. This was probably something freegans learned to do by instinct: cover their tracks. "This way," he said, leading me toward that little office in the back of the warehouse.

The floor was uneven—warped wooden slats covered with a dried brown paste of that pigeon and/or bat poop. I was wearing new-ish tennis shoes, but I could feel the loose nails and broken glass dried into the paste on the floor even through my thick rubber soles.

Of course the glass office windows were broken, and someone had also yanked the door off its hinges. But they'd left the big blocky desk in place along with a dented metal cabinet of some sort along the wall.

Wade smiled, then opened the doors on the cabinet. It was packed with stuff, but not the kind of stuff I expected. It wasn't yellowed papers or soggy ledgers. There were cardboard boxes full of paperbacks, and a rolled-up bedspread, and a gym bag, and more boxes full of clothing—t-shirts and hoodies and jeans and socks and undies. There was even an iPod and a computer monitor—more than a couple of years out of date.

"This is yours," I said. His personal possessions. Somehow it just seemed obvious.

"Everything I own," he said.

"I thought most freegans sold all their stuff, or gave it away in freegan stores."

"They do."

"But you were supposed to go away to college in the fall, so you brought your stuff here?"

He shook his head. "No. I had a place to store my stuff for the summer. It's when fall rolled around that I moved it here—took me forever on a bike, by the way. I couldn't afford a storage locker, and I figured this place was so old that everyone would think there isn't anything left worth looting. At first, it was just temporary. What if I changed my mind? What if I didn't like the freegan lifestyle?"

I nodded. That all made perfect sense.

"But then when I realized I liked being a freegan, I also realized I liked having it here."

"Just knowing it was safe," I said.

He looked at me. "Yeah." He rolled his eyes. "Geez, I go on and on about being a freegan, about changing the world, but I can't even tell my family. And I talk about not having any possessions, about being so 'free,' and here I have my secret stash. I really am a hypocrite, aren't I?"

"No!" I blurted. "No. I don't think it makes you a hypocrite at all. I think it makes you human." More than anything, it made me like him.

"Yeah?" he said.

The wood floor creaked under my feet. "Yeah."

Was Wade blushing? With his dark skin, I couldn't tell.

"Someday someone'll probably steal it," he said. "Then again, I probably won't even know. This is actually the first time I've come back here since I left it here a year and a half ago."

"Really?" I said.

"I've never even told anyone. Not any of the other freegans. You're the first."

I didn't know what to say. True confessions? I was touched that he'd shared this hidden part of himself with me. Suddenly, I wanted to share my secrets with him, but I didn't really have any, except the one about how fast I was falling for this strange, complicated guy. Oh, and the fact that I fell for guys.

"Wade?" I said.

But right then the doorway to the warehouse squeaked open. It was so much louder than I ever would've expected, like a hundred seagulls squawking. A new ray of sunlight flashed across the floor, lighting the swirling dust that we'd kicked up just by walking across the warehouse.

My eyes met Wade's.

"I know you're in here!" said a voice. "I saw you break inside!"

Wade held his finger up to his lips. Then, not hesitating at all, he whispered, "Follow me."

"Where?" I whispered back, a little frantically. "He'll see us!"

"No, he won't. It'll take a minute for his eyes to adjust to the dark. Trust me." This sounded like exactly the kind of thing that someone who spent a lot of time breaking into abandoned buildings would know. So I did trust him.

Easing the cabinet closed behind him, Wade stepped out into the main warehouse. He moved so smoothly, like a train on a track, like a duck gliding across a lake. The floor barely creaked under his feet, but it sounded like the wailing of sirens under mine—and, of course, the pigeon and/or bat poop crunched. How had I not noticed before how loud it was to walk across this floor?

Wade quickly strode—floated?—straight to that rusted metal barrel and ducked down behind it. I followed behind, but not like a train or a duck. We both peeked out around the same side of the barrel. I could smell the sweat from Wade's smooth brown neck. He smelled like salt and blackberries with just a hint of pine—real pine, not some fake cologne. How in the world did someone smell this good without deodorant? And what in the world was I doing noticing a thing like that at a time like this?

"I know you're in here!" said the voice. All I saw was a silhouette standing in the doorway, but I could tell that Wade's plan had worked: his head was looking over at the office where we'd been, the place where we seemed most likely to be, not at the rusty barrel where we were hiding now. Who was this anyway? One of the neighboring business owners charged with keeping an eye on the warehouse? And what if he had a gun?

Wade looked back at me and once again, held his finger up to his lips. I said I'd wanted adventure, but not like this. I'd been thinking more of the bare-feet-in-the-surf kind.

The figure in the doorway started across the floor of the warehouse, his steps squeaking even louder than mine. But he was walking for the office, not for where we were hiding.

"I mean it!" the voice said. "I know you're in here!"

As the man traversed the floor, Wade and I instinctively maneuvered our way around the barrel, always keeping him on the opposite side of us. I was sort of proud of myself for picking this up so quickly, but even now, the floor under Wade was barely squeaking, but the floor under me still was.

Once the man was halfway to the office, Wade nodded to me again, then bolted for the closest wooden pillar.

The man stopped once and glanced over our way. The pillar was narrower than the barrel, and presumably the man's eyes had adjusted to the dark by now, so Wade and I pushed ourselves even closer together, trying to conform to the shape of the wooden post.

His musk was even stronger now, and his body was lean and hard. I'd held lean and hard guys before—both Kevin and Otto are lean and hard. But there was a different kind of hardness to Wade's body. Everything wasn't just in the right place, it was also slightly exaggerated, bigger than I was used to: wider shoulders, thicker arms, rounder ass (which I, of course, made a point not to touch with my crotch). But the waist was just as narrow, maybe narrower.

The man hesitated for only a second, just sort of glancing over at us. Then he started toward the office again.

"Come on!" he said. "Show yourselves!"

Wade nodded to the next pillar closest to the open door. On one hand, I understood the predicament we were in—like I said, this man could have a gun. But on the other hand, I confess I was enjoying the feel of Wade's body and the smell of his musk. (I was enjoying it a little too much, if you must know. I was worried Wade was going to back into me, and let's just say that was no banana in my pocket. Again, I ask: how could I be thinking of a thing like that at a time like this?)

Breathlessly, we reached the next pillar. Now we were a lot closer to the open doorway than we were to the guy over by the office. He wasn't looking back at us at all now.

So with one more nod, Wade and I ran for the open garage door. But Wade stopped. Now he was the silhouette, at least from the perspective of the guy back in the warehouse.

"You there!" he called in a deep, scary voice that didn't sound anything like the one I knew. "Get out of that warehouse right now!" I knew right away that the whole point of this was to distract the man from the office, so he wouldn't find Wade's things in the cabinet.

Sure enough, the man turned.

"Go!" Wade said to me, and we ran toward our bikes in the trees. Fortunately, they were still there, so we jumped on them and rode. I was all set to ride off down the street, but Wade said, "No! Here!" He pulled his bike off the road and onto one of the legs of the abandoned rail line. It was an awkward, bumpy ride over weeds and rail ties, but almost immediately I saw the point of it: if the man in the warehouse had a car, he couldn't follow us here. I wished I'd thought of it.

The adrenaline kept pumping through me long after we were away from the warehouse (it even took a long time for me to lose that banana in my pocket!). I couldn't remember the last time I'd felt so alive. Turns out I wanted more than bare-feet-in-the-surf after all.

"Hey, you hungry?" Wade said out of the blue.

I *was* hungry, but, um, I wasn't interested in eating out of a garbage can.

Wade laughed at my expression. "That's not what I meant."

"What?"

"You thought I was asking if you wanted to eat out of a Dumpster."

Busted.

"No…" I said.

"It's okay. It makes sense. But I just meant that you could join us for dinner at the freegan house."

"Oh."

"You want to?"

I hesitated, but I'm not sure why. I'd spent the afternoon with Wade. I wasn't worried about not being able to trust him. On the contrary, suddenly I was desperate to smell his sweat again, to inhale that mix of salt and blackberry and pine. I wanted the scent of him on me, wanted it soaking so deep I couldn't wash him out of my clothes or off my skin.

"Come on," he said. "Life is an adventure, right?"

I was already texting my parents, telling them I wouldn't be home for dinner.

CHAPTER EIGHT

The other freegans were barbecuing in the back-yard behind their house, with a grill that looked like they'd made themselves from salvaged bricks and chicken wire.

"Russel!" Venus said, running over to greet me with a bear hug. "You're back! I wasn't sure I'd ever see you again."

"Me too," I said. "But I was hoping I would. Wow, that smells good." I meant the barbecue, which did smell incredible. Rather than briquettes, they were burning actual wood—a broken chair, I think.

"Isn't it great?" Venus said, swaying in the court-yard. "Come on, I'll introduce you."

The first time I'd been here, I hadn't met anyone else. Meeting them now, I sort of expected them to all have off-beat names like Soupcan or Boxcar or, well,

Venus. But it turned out they were just Rick, Gilly, Jill, and Matthew.

They greeted me with nods. No one shook my hand even though I sort of expected them to, and I wondered if that was a freegan thing—don't do what most people do, don't give into mainstream expectations.

"Let's eat!" said Matthew, sort of a scruffy geek with dirty blond hair (*literally* dirty). A couple of people left for the kitchen and returned with plates and forks and two big bowls—one with a salad and another with brown rice. Then they dished up the barbecue, which was being cooked on wooden skewers.

"Is this the wild greens salad you promised me?" I said to Venus when she handed me a plate.

"It *is!*" she said, beaming. "Oh! But there aren't any nettles!"

"It's okay. I think that's sort of advance level anyway."

I tasted the salad. It was amazing. It wasn't like one you'd buy in the store or eat in a restaurant. There must have been six different plants, and every one of them tasted different from the others. They were more intense than lettuce—more bitter or more leafy or more spicy, and always more flavorful. Each leaf somehow seemed more *real*, like you could actually taste the exact spot of ground where it had grown. It didn't even need dressing, though someone had drizzled something tangy over it.

I slid the meat off the skewers. It was still sizzling it was so hot off the fire. It surprised me a little, that they were having barbecue. For some reason, I'd thought the freegans would all be vegetarians.

I tasted it. "It's good. But it's different. Not beef, not chicken. What is it?" It was meaty without being fatty.

"Fox," Mark said.

Was he joking? They were barbecuing fox?

"Where did you get...?"

Wade suddenly squirmed in his rickety lawn chair. "It's roadkill. Ah, I totally should've told you that, shouldn't I? Especially after you said you didn't want to eat out of a Dumpster. I'm sorry, Russel—I didn't even think about that. This is all just so normal to us."

I wasn't sure whether to spit or swallow the bite in my mouth. In the end, I swallowed. "You eat road-kill?"

"It's not what you think!" Venus said. "We only use it when we're totally sure it's absolutely fresh."

"How can you be sure it's fresh?"

"All kinds of ways. The eyes, for one thing. They have to be clear, not white or clouded—that means it just died. But also the smell. And how stiff the body is. Even whether or not it still has fleas!"

"Fleas?"

"Actually," Wade said, still not meeting my eyes, "roadkill can be a lot fresher than the meat you buy in the store. Remember, even meat you buy in a grocery store isn't frozen right away. And it can be weeks or months before it actually hits your table, so they pump it full of chemicals or dyes just to fool you into thinking it's fresh. With roadkill, you can at least judge for yourself whether or not it's fresh."

Was this true? What they were saying did sort of make sense. Or was this just more propaganda from a cult?

"You don't have to finish it," Wade said. His deep brown eyes poured into mine again at last. "Seriously. We don't ever want to force people to do something they don't want to do. That's what the rest of the culture tries to do to us. That's the exact opposite of what freeganism is all about."

I looked down at the meat on my plate. I knew that everyone was watching me even if they were pretending not to, but that's not why I took another bite.

Wade smiled, and Venus squealed.

"You wanna try the raccoon?" Jill said, over at the grill, holding up another skewer.

"Raccoon?" I said.

"It's not as good as the fox—not by a long shot."

"People actually eat raccoons?" I said.

"You've never been to the South, have you?" Wade said. "Everyone eats raccoons down there."

This time, everyone stared at me openly, curious to see what I'd do.

"Hell, yes!" I said, reaching for the skewer and digging in. Venus actually cheered.

It was gamier and stringier than the fox, but you know what? It was seasoned with a generous shaking of spontaneity.

Okay, that was clunky. The point is it was exciting to be doing something new and different and unexpected. Neurotic, guilt-ridden, self-conscious me was finally cutting loose! Soon somebody was going to have to scrape me down off the ceiling with a broom.

After dinner in the yard, we all went inside to play Monopoly—ironically, with rules that were both hilarious and subversive. You "won" the game by being the first person to give away all your money and houses and hotels, but there were specific rules: (1) you had to be on the same square as someone else in order to give them something, and (2) you couldn't give anything to anyone who had more than you. You also did the opposite of what the little Chance and Community Chest cards told you to do. Oh, and you could also hop trains to any other railroad on the board.

It was surprisingly challenging and a lot of fun (I'm sure the dandelion wine didn't hurt).

But as we laughed and played, I couldn't help but think about what my parents would do if they found out where I was—that I was playing Ironic Monopoly with a bunch of homeless people in an empty house they were squatting in—er, occupying. Or if they knew I'd spent the afternoon rooting around abandoned buildings and had just finished a dinner of barbecued roadkill.

They'd be totally shocked and appalled. They'd yank me from that house so fast it would pull my ear off.

And it wasn't just my parents. It was *most* parents. They'd totally flip out. I'm not one to paint things in extreme terms, but I don't think I'm exaggerating when I say that most adults would take one look at this freegan house and their heads would literally explode—I mean, blood and brains everywhere.

But it was funny. These people they'd be so upset about? They were sitting around playing board games after dinner rather than watching TV. And that dinner? They'd cooked it themselves—roadkill, yes, but also with fresh vegetables, some of which they'd gathered themselves, and *brown rice*. Have you ever known a teenager to eat brown rice? Except for Min (obviously not typical), I hadn't. And they'd all cleaned up afterward. "We're all in this together," Wade had said, and it didn't just apply to the meals. The freegans had some pretty out-there beliefs, but the fact is they cared about the world and the people in it. They weren't hurting anyone—it sure seemed like they were even helping people. Basically, they gave a damn. And they were living life—that was impossible to deny.

Boy, was I totally drinking the Kool-Aid or what? But honestly, what exactly was it these guys were doing that was such a bad thing?

Before too long, I checked my phone and realized I was already late.

"I should go," I said to Wade.

Venus overheard me. "Really? Noooo!"

"Well, it's a school night," I said, feeling stupid even as I said it. The truth is it felt like the exact opposite of a school night. It felt like no day or night I'd ever spent in my whole entire life.

"I'll walk you to your bike," Wade said, and so he did.

Outside, I slipped on my helmet, but lingered. "Thanks," I said.

"For what?" Wade asked.

"For a really, really great day."

He smiled in the dark. "I'm glad you liked it."

Why did this feel like the end of a date? Because that's what it was, right? Come on, validate my reality here!

"Will I see you again?" Wade said.

"I hope so." I hesitated. "I'd give you my phone number, but…"

He nodded. "I don't have a phone. On the other hand, you know where I live."

"And I know which Dumpsters you hang out in."

He smiled again—a full-fledged grin. The wind blew and I thought I smelled the faintest hint of salt and blackberry and pine—but then it was gone. *Had* it been a date, or had I misinterpreted the whole thing? I wanted to kiss him, but I felt stupid. What if he wasn't out to the other freegans and they spotted us out in the yard? What if he wasn't even gay? And part of me, a stubborn part, thought, "He's two years older than I am—why can't he be the one to kiss *me?*" (Another part of me, I guess a slightly racist part, thought, What's it's like to kiss a black guy? Does it feel any different?)

He hesitated, smiling, and I hesitated, not smiling. But no one made a move. So finally I climbed onto the bike. "Well," I said. "Thanks again."

"Sure thing, Russel. See you around."

I didn't look back, but I could tell he watched me ride down the street.

Night had fallen, and I suppose the air was cold on my bike ride home, but I didn't feel it. I also didn't care that we hadn't kissed. I couldn't stop thinking about Wade and the day I'd had, reliving every moment.

I have no idea how all this is sounding, if the afternoon Wade and I had spent together seems at all romantic to you. I mean, it was mostly just the two of us having a conversation about philosophy, then breaking into an abandoned warehouse with pigeon and/or bat poop, and eating barbecued roadkill with a side of dandelion salad.

So if it doesn't sound romantic, you'll just have to take my word for it, because it totally, TOTALLY was.

CHAPTER NINE

What a day I'd had! I was dying to tell someone about it.

I still didn't want to talk to Min or Gunnar about Wade. Even now, I was embarrassed by the whole "forsaking love" thing.

So I IMed Otto.

Smuggler: Hello you.

OttoManEmpire: Hello you.

Smuggler: It's possible I'm in love.

OttoManEmpire: What? Who? This Wade guy?

Smuggler: Yes. He's amazing. And I think he might like me back.

OttoManEmpire: Tell me! Tell me everything!

So I did, from the way Wade had been waiting for me at the Dumpster, to the expedition to the warehouse, to the meal of roadkill and wild greens salad, to the game of Ironic Monopoly, to the almost-kiss by the bike.

Smuggler: I'm crazy, aren't I? I mean, this is more star-crossed than that movie about the vampire in love with the werewolf. He's a homeless person.

OttoManEmpire: He's a freegan! It's totally different.

Smuggler: How do you know?

OttoManEmpire: I've been doing some research. They sound really cool.

Smuggler: But still! It's like the movie about the woman in love with a ghost! Or the book about the man who falls in love with himself from another time-line!

OttoManEmpire: You're being melodramatic. It's absolutely nothing like any of that.

Smuggler: I know. But it's fun to be melodramatic every now and then.

OttoManEmpire: What are you going to do?

Smuggler: Can I be honest?

OttoManEmpire: Do you really need to ask that?

Smuggler: I think I'm going to go for it.

OttoManEmpire: Good. Because I would've been COMPLETELY disappointed if you didn't!

The next afternoon during a break, Gunnar pulled me into an alcove in the school hallway.

"So," he said. "I've learned some interesting things about Kevin."

"What?" I said.

"Kevin? You know, the guy you used to date? The one you asked me to spy on?"

"Gunnar! I didn't ask you to *spy* on him!" Okay, maybe I had. But he didn't need to put it exactly like that, especially not where someone—Kevin! or Min—

could overhear. I lowered my voice to a whisper. "Anyway, it doesn't matter. I don't care about Kevin anymore." I *didn't* care. Wade was the new guy in my life—or at least I hoped he would be.

"You don't care about Kevin?" Gunnar said. "Last weekend, you cared—you cared a lot. What changed between last weekend and today?"

I still wasn't ready to tell Gunnar about Wade. So instead, I said, "Nothing. I just changed my mind."

"That's too bad, because I've learned some interesting stuff."

"That's great. But like I said, I don't think I want to know it. Gunnar, I'm really sorry I got you involved, and I'm really impressed you took it so seriously, but it was a mistake."

"I took some photos too."

"Photos?" This was so like Gunnar—I should have known he would have gotten obsessed. I was an absolute fool to have gone to him with a favor like this. "Like I said, that's great. But it was wrong to ask you. So let's just pretend that I never—"

He started flipping through the photos on his phone, all the ones he'd taken of Kevin earlier in the week. Right away, he came to a shot taken of someone standing in the shower in the school locker room. I couldn't be absolutely sure it was Kevin, because he was facing away. But—how do I put this delicately? It looked a lot like Kevin, especially his ass (which is terrific, if you must know).

"Gunnar!" I said, horrified. I pulled him and the phone close to make sure no one else could see its face.

"What?" he said casually.

"You took pictures of Kevin in the shower?!" But even now, and as embarrassing as this is to admit, I didn't look away from the photo. I'd totally forgotten what an amazing ass Kevin had (okay, not really).

"Why not?" he said. I knew that Gunnar wasn't turned on by the pictures. As long as I'd known him, I'd been certain he was completely, totally straight. For him, secretly observing Kevin had just been another project.

"Well, for one thing, it's illegal!" I said. "For about ten different reasons! And it's total invasion of his privacy! What if you lost your phone? What if you accidentally emailed or texted these photos to someone?"

Gunnar scrolled one picture over. It was another shot of Kevin in the shower, but this time Kevin had turned around. He was shampooing his hair, so he clearly didn't see Gunnar. But the picture itself was full-frontal. And as amazing as Kevin looked from behind, he looked even better from the front.

"*Gunnar!*" I said, even more horrified than before. "Delete these right now!"

Yes, yes, even now, I wasn't looking away. And there were people passing in the hallway not five feet away.

"*Right* now?" Gunnar said, simpering. He was toying with me. But even now, even after Gunnar had totally busted me for staring at these pictures that I was hypocritically insisting he delete, I couldn't look away.

"I just learned some things about Kevin that I think you should hear," he said.

"Okay, okay!" I said. "I'll listen! But first delete these pictures!"

"Are you *sure*?"

"Yes, I'm sure! Do it now!" I reached for the phone to delete them myself, but he dodged my grip.

"You don't want me to email you copies?"

"*Gunnar!*"

"Okay, okay!" His mouth was a vortex of smirks and grins, but I watched as he deleted the naked photos.

It was only after he was done that I realized how hard my blood was pumping. (And yes, the truth is I totally did wish he had emailed me copies first.)

"Well, it was a little surprising," he said.

"What was?" I said.

"Kevin."

"What?"

"I'm telling you what I learned about Kevin." I must have looked at him blankly, because he added, "You promised that if I deleted the photos, you'd listen to what I learned about Kevin. Like, two seconds ago?"

"Okay, right. Yeah."

"So, anyway, Kevin," he said. "At first I was surprised by how boring he is."

"Boring?"

"I don't know. After the way you and Min turned on him last year, I figured that he was some kind of monster, you know? But he's not a monster. In fact, he's really a nice guy. Boring, but nice. At one point, he literally helped a little old lady—not across the street, but he carried her groceries to her car at the supermarket."

So Gunnar hadn't just taken photos of Kevin in the locker room at school—he'd actually followed him off-campus? What kind of Frankenstein's Monster had I created—and how far did his rampage stretch?

"Hey," I said. "You didn't post those pictures of Kevin to your blog or anything, did you?"

"No," he said. "I'm not a complete idiot, and shut up and listen, because this is important: Kevin's not a jerk."

"What?"

"No, seriously. He's a nice guy. I like him. He does volunteer work with kids with autism." So Kevin had Gunnar's approval? On one hand, this was what I'd been wanting to hear earlier in the week. But on the other hand, I was interested in Wade now. Right?

"Well?" he said.

"Well what?" I said.

"Are you going to give him another chance?"

I sighed. "I honestly don't know."

"Because if *you're* not going to date him, *I* will!"

I rolled my eyes.

"What? The guy's a total catch! And man, what a body. I mean, I'm straight, but I'm not blind. You really tapped that, huh?"

"Gunnar!"

"What?"

"Look," I said. "I know Kevin's not a jerk. He's even friends with Brian Bund."

"Well, not anymore."

I looked at Gunnar.

"Yeah, that was one weird thing," he said, remembering. "It happened just this morning. Kevin and Brian got into this argument in the parking lot right near me. Kevin accused him of stealing something, called him a loser. He actually was kind of a jerk about it."

"Really?" I said. This couldn't be right: Brian would never steal anything.

Gunnar nodded.

Why would Kevin make an accusation that wasn't true? Because maybe he wasn't such a Boy Scout after all? It would figure. Maybe that thing in the park wasn't so out of character. Or maybe he had some kind of Jekyll and Hyde thing going on.

The bell rang for class, and Gunnar started to leave.

"Wait!" I said, and he looked at me. "What does any of this have to do with those photos you showed me of Kevin in the shower?"

"What?"

"Those naked photos of Kevin. They don't have anything to do with any of the things you just told me."

"Yeah, I know. I just led with those to get you hooked." When I stared at him, confused, he added, "You didn't wanna hear what I had to say! You really think I was going to do all that spying on Kevin for nothing?"

CHAPTER TEN

That Friday, Min, Gunnar, and I broke into Leah's house.

I still thought it was a *terrible* idea, but Min was desperate for answers about whatever secret Leah was keeping—plus, she'd invoked the "friend" bat-signal—so Gunnar and I had no choice but to go along. That said, it meant I'd participated in two break-ins in the course of a single week: the warehouse with Wade and now this. Suddenly, I was living a full-fledged life of crime. What was next—elaborate cons involving the school's football uniforms? Tunneling into the principal's office from the classroom next door?

I know I'd said I'd wanted adventure, but this was ridiculous.

We gathered beforehand in Min's bedroom. The room is pretty dark—dark paint, navy bedspread—and she has a big poster of the planet Earth on a wall and a mobile of Jupiter and its moons hanging from the ceiling, so visiting her there is a little like walking into deep space.

"So tell us your plan, Millicent Min, Girl Genius," I said. This was my new nickname for Min, taken from this book we'd both loved, *Millicent Min, Girl Genius*, about an over-achieving Asian-American girl. But Millicent in the book had just been an uptight genius, not a jealous lunatic like my Min.

Sure enough, Min said, "No."

"What do you mean 'no'?" I said. "You're not going to tell us the plan?"

"No, but don't worry. I've got it all figured out. Trust me."

I rolled my eyes. Then I looked at Gunnar. He stared at Min like an adoring puppy. In other words, he was totally eating up this whole secret spy thing. I didn't even bother trying to enlist him into my demand for details.

First, Min had us dress all in black. Not cat-burglar black: Goth black, with lots of make-up and painted-on tattoos. This way the dark clothes would make us invisible to the residents, but if we happened to get caught by police or security guards, it wouldn't look like we were thieves, but just a bunch of kids who'd stumbled somewhere we didn't belong.

I had to give Min full credit for this: it was pretty clever.

We waited until it was dark, then told Min's parents we were going to a costume party (in February?) and drove over to where Leah lived, this gated community on the outskirts of town. It was called Cranberry Creek, but there were no cranberries or even a creek—just a bunch of big, expensive houses. We parked outside, and the gate itself was easy enough to get around: we just had to climb this stone fence and sneak through someone's backyard.

Leah's parents' house was even bigger than the other houses: they were really, really rich. It was one of those sprawling suburban mansions that seems to be all garage doors. It had been built up against a hillside, and the perfectly pruned yard was thick with trees and shrubs. That was the good news, at least from a breaking-in perspective. The bad news was the whole thing was lit up like a carnival, with porch lights and driveway lights and yard lights in rows along the pathways.

"It's fine," Min said. "Leah told me her whole family is away visiting her mom's sister for the night."

But by now even Gunnar was having second thoughts. "A house like that, I'm sure it has a serious security system," he said.

Min's eyes never left the house. "It does. But the windows are only alarmed on the first floor, and the motion detectors are in the stairwell."

"How are we going to get to the windows on the second floor?" I said. "Levitate?"

She looked at me and smiled. "Trust me."

I didn't say what I was thinking, which was if the police caught us inside the yard or house, they'd call my parents, Goth outfits or not. Then I'd be totally grounded for weeks, if not months, and by the time I had any freedom again, Wade would have left town for the big city. If I was grounded, I wouldn't even have any way to let him know.

My relationship with him would be over before it had even begun.

But Min was one of my two best friends. It had taken me a while, but I'd finally learned that my friendships with her and Gunnar were far and away the most important things in my life—more important than any potential boyfriend, that's for sure. Basically, I'd do anything for them. So if my helping Min meant possibly losing my shot with Wade, so be it.

We climbed up the tree closest to the house. It hung out over the roof, so we were able to jump down right onto the shingles. Then we scrambled up toward the chimney. At first I couldn't figure out what the hell Min was thinking: were we going to pull a Santa Claus? But she was wearing a black backpack from which she pulled out a sturdy rope. At one end was a very secure lasso that she threw around the chimney. The other end was firmly tied to a lifejacket that Min slipped on and snapped into place.

"The window to Leah's bedroom is right below us," Min said. "Lower me down."

"Lower you *down*?" I said. "Min, this is crazy! Crazy

and dangerous!"

"You're doing a really crappy job of trusting me, you know that?"

"Won't it be locked?" Gunnar asked, meaning the window below us.

"When I was here the other day, I made sure to leave it open just a crack when Leah's back was turned. Once I'm inside, I'll take off the life jacket and yank on the rope. You guys pull it back up, and Russel, you follow me down."

"Wait," Gunnar said. "Why Russ?"

"Yeah!" I said. "Why me?"

"Because you're lighter. Besides, Gunnar, I need you to keep a lookout here on the roof. Hide behind the chimney, and if you see anyone coming, call us on our cell phones. Speaking of which, put your phones on vibrate now."

I knew another reason Min had picked me to come with her was because she needed someone who could stay focused, which was not necessarily Gunnar's strong suit.

Gunnar and I lowered Min down to the bedroom window. Fortunately, Leah's window looked out from the back side of the house. I could see a pool and hot tub down below us. There were plenty of bright lights in the pool area, meaning we'd be very visible from down below. But as long as there was no one home, we were okay.

Once Min was inside the bedroom, I followed her

down, hanging like a spider on a web until I somehow managed to scramble my way in through the open window.

I looked at Min in the dark of the room. "It worked!" The subtext to this was: "We didn't kill ourselves!"

"You sound surprised," she said.

"Truthfully? I kind of am." This whole break-in plan was incredibly stupid—pointless, reckless, and wildly irresponsible. But I had to admit that as incredibly stupid plans go, it was kinda brilliant.

Min handed me a flashlight—she never did turn on the lights—and I aimed the beam around the room. Leah had lots of books, figurines of dragons and monsters on her shelves, and old movie posters on the walls.

Min, meanwhile, was already single-mindedly rifling through her desk.

"What do I do?" I asked.

"Look in the closet."

So I did.

It was a walk-in—a *big* walk-in. Hanging clothes were jammed in tightly on both sides of the closet, but it was kind of funny: the clothes on one side were mostly bright colors, pink and blue and red and yellow, sometimes with frills and lace; and the clothes on the other side were all dark, drab grays and browns and military green. I didn't know Leah very well, but I knew she was closeted at her school. I couldn't help but wonder if her actual closet reflected something about her being *in* the closet, about how she'd created two completely different personalities: her girly-girl self, the role she played at her school, and her real geeky self, the way she was around Min and me.

There was a dresser in the closet, and I opened the drawers, but it was just underwear and socks and t-shirts and swimsuits.

A stack of frayed cardboard boxes leaned against the wall in the back of the closet. I figured that was more promising than clothing, so I started looking through them. Mostly they were shoes, but there were also sweaters and papers and books. It felt weird, wrong, going through someone else's things without their permission—sort of like taking photos of some-one naked in the shower, exactly what I'd been so up-set with Gunnar about. Before, when I'd vowed to do whatever one of my best friends wanted me to do, I hadn't thought about this.

I found a yellow plastic bag alongside the card-board boxes. Inside were balloons and streamers and party hats and candles, all still in their wrappers. They were party supplies for a birthday that clearly hadn't happened yet.

There were also buttons personalized with Min's face on them. "Happy Birthday Min!" they said.

I carried the bag out to Min, still frantically going through Leah's desk. She barely looked up.

"Min," I said. "Your birthday's coming up in two

weeks, right?"

She still didn't look at me. "So?"

"I think I found something." I opened the bag and showed the contents to Min.

She didn't say anything for a second. She reached down and picked up one of the buttons with her face on it.

"Don't you see?" I said. "She's planning a birthday party. A *surprise* birthday party. For you. That's what she's been hiding." So now it was the Elephant of Surprise Parties. It had all been a simple misunderstanding, like the plot of some stupid old sitcom.

Finally, she looked me in the eye. "Wouldn't she have invited you?"

"Maybe she just hasn't done it yet. Maybe she was worried about me—or Gunnar—spilling the beans. But doesn't she have a bunch of friends from her school that you sometimes hang out with? Maybe it's for you and them. Didn't you say she liked it when you did stuff with them? I bet that's the phone call she was making at the pizza place. She looked guilty because she wasn't going to invite me to the party."

Min melted into her chair.

"She loves me," Min said. "Of course she does. I'm such an idiot." She started to sob. I'd never seen Min cry before, and the whole concept was sort of rocking my world. Min was the Spock of Goodkind High School: her general braininess and seeming lack of emotion was just a plot device to make *you* feel more emotional when she finally spilled hers.

"Min?" I said, kneeling down next to her. "Min, listen to me. You let your imagination get the best of you. So what? You had a moment of insecurity. Big deal. It just means you're human. Maybe you even talked me into doing something incredibly stupid and wildly irresponsible."

She flashed me a glare that would dry paint.

"Sorry, I couldn't resist," I said. "The point is it's okay. None of this matters. You wanted answers, and you got them, and now Leah doesn't ever even need to know that you had this little moment of doubt."

"Really?" she said.

I smiled. "Trust *me*. But let's just get out of here before we do get caught."

She nodded even as she wiped a tear.

But of course that's the exact moment that my phone started vibrating. It was Gunnar calling from the roof.

"There's someone coming!" he hissed.

"What?" I said. "Who?" My panic button had definitely been pushed.

"I don't know! But there's a car driving into the driveway right now!"

I clicked off my phone. "We have to go," I said to Min. "Now." I turned for the lifejacket at the end of the rope. "You first."

"No, you should—"

"Don't argue! Just do it!"

But Gunnar hadn't even pulled her halfway up when I heard the rumble of the garage door opening underneath me. Up on the roof, Min fumbled her way out of the harness. But by the time she dropped it back down to me, I heard the beep of the burglar alarm being deactivated from the room down below.

Whoever it was, they were home and inside the house. But I could still work my way up to the roof. It wasn't like whoever this was would be going out into the backyard, which is the only place where they'd be able to see me.

"We don't even need to get in the pool," said a voice in the room below—a man's voice. "Just the hot tub. Come on, it'll feel good."

They were going for a swim—which meant they'd be in the backyard after all! Who was this anyway? Did Leah have an older brother who decided to come home from college for the weekend?

"It feels weird," a voice said—a female voice. "I mean, what if your wife comes home?"

"I told you, everyone's gone for the night," the first voice said. "Besides, you were the one who wanted to see where I live."

Wait. This was Leah's dad? He'd come up with an excuse to stay home while the rest of the family went off on an out-of-town visit. When the cat's away, the mouse will have sex with his secretary? Or is that "rat"?

Still, I thought, maybe this could work to my advantage. Now that Leah's dad had turned off the burglar alarm, I could sneak my way out the front door while they were out in the pool.

The girl said something else, but I couldn't make it out.

Leah's dad laughed. "Well, it's not like it's anything I haven't seen before."

"I don't care. It just feels weird."

"Hold on. I have one you can borrow."

"I'm not wearing your wife's swimsuit!"

"It won't be my wife's. Trust me, that'd be way too big for you."

I froze. Leah's dad was offering to lend his girlfriend a swimsuit—but not one of his wife's. Didn't that mean he was borrowing one of Leah's? If it did, it meant he might be coming into the bedroom to get it. He'd catch me for sure!

Footsteps thundered up the stairs.

Terrified, I glanced around the room. There wasn't enough space under the desk to hide. I started for the bed, but quickly saw it was too close to the floor—there wasn't enough room for me there either.

The floor creaked as he walked down the hallway.

As quietly as possible, I darted for the walk-in closet and closed the door behind me.

I was actually hiding in a *closet*? Did anyone in the history of the world ever stay effectively hidden in a closet? With everything packed so tightly together, I couldn't even hide behind the clothes. And the boxes next to the dresser weren't big enough to hide behind either.

The dresser! Leah kept her swimsuits in that dresser!

Without thinking, I yanked open the drawer, grabbed a swimsuit, and threw it out onto the floor right in front of the closet. Then I quickly eased the closet door closed behind me again.

I crouched down in the corner of the closet as the bedroom door squeaked open. Leah's dad was now just outside.

I held my breath. Would Leah's dad see the swimsuit on the floor? If he turned on the overhead light, he might. But if he headed straight for the closet—if he planned to just turn on the overhead light in here— he'd see me for sure. And even if he *did* see it on the floor, would he grab it and bring it down to his girlfriend? I mean, she'd probably want a *clean* suit, not one Leah had presumably just been wearing. Then again, how would she know? And a man who cheated on his wife was pretty clearly someone who didn't have big issues with honesty.

The overhead light in the bedroom didn't turn on. The floor creaked. He was coming closer.

Just outside the bedroom door, Leah's dad stopped. I could see his shadow under the door from the lights in the backyard. I could also hear him breathing. It was like he was right next me, like we were trapped inside the same dark coffin. Weirdly, it wasn't hard to keep on holding my breath. Under the circumstances, breathing just wasn't that high a priority.

Then I remembered something else: the bedroom window. Had I remembered to close it? Had Leah's dad seen it and realized that something was up?

Finally, the shadow under the door shifted: he was either picking up the suit or he was stepping toward the closet.

If you're already holding your breath, is it possible to hold your breath *harder*? Because that's what I was doing. At the same time, a wave of sweat broke out over my body. I was suddenly wet all over, even in unusual places, like between my toes. I'd never sweated so badly in my life—my clothes were suddenly soaked, like I'd been caught in a rainstorm. It was the weirdest thing.

But the closet door didn't open. It was the bedroom door that opened back up. Leah's dad stopped breathing in my ear as he left the room. He must have grabbed the suit on the floor.

The floor of the upstairs hallway squeaked as Leah's dad plodded away, then the steps thundered, but I still didn't move. It wasn't until I heard the splash of water in the backyard that I slowly crept out of the closet. I glanced over at the window and saw that I'd remembered to close it after all.

I texted Gunnar and Min on the roof, telling them that I was going to try to sneak out the front door and to meet me in the yard.

Then I headed for the stairs.

It was funny: I'd been happy before to hear the creak of Leah's dad's footsteps in the hallway, and the thump of his feet on the steps, because they'd given me some warning that he was coming. But now I was dying a thousand deaths when I was the one creaking down that hallway and squeaking down those steps.

When I reached the foyer, I glanced back through the house to the pool in back. Leah's dad and his girlfriend were both in the hot tub now, and it looked like the swimsuits were already coming off. So much for modesty—but I suspect that suit had been important to the woman because it meant she wasn't a slut or something (full disclosure: heterosexuals confuse me).

I quietly eased the front door open and slipped out into the yard. At first I was a little freaked out by all the lights—stepping onto that front porch was a little like setting foot on a stage. But once the door was closed behind me, unless someone had actually *seen* me coming out that door, I now had plausible deniability that I had ever been in the house in the first place.

I met Min and Gunnar who were hiding in the bushes, and together we hurried back to where Min's car was parked.

Once we were safely inside the car, Min went off with a string of apologies to Gunnar and me both—about how she had been certain that everyone would be gone and how she'd been stupid to be so suspicious of Leah in the first place. I let her go on a bit because, well, it really had been an incredibly stupid, wildly irresponsible plan (even if it was kind of clever too). It seemed like Min did sort of owe Gunnar and me an apology, especially since I'd come so close to getting caught.

But you want to know the truth? I wasn't really that annoyed. In fact, I would have done the break-in all over again, even if I'd known there was a chance I could get caught at the end. The fact is, my life finally had some genuine excitement—some of that adventure I'd been pining for.

And I was absolutely loving it.

CHAPTER ELEVEN

The next day, Saturday, I went to see Wade again. If I really was going to choose between Kevin and him, I didn't see any reason why I shouldn't learn more about him—like if he really was gay, for one thing (that seemed important to know). Plus, he'd said he was leaving town soon. I wanted to tell him how I felt about him—and give him a chance to say how he felt about me!—before that happened.

I obviously couldn't call or text, so I just rode my bike over to the freegan house and went up to the front door and knocked.

Venus answered the door. "Russel!" she said. She hugged me, and I hugged her back, and then she said, "You want Wade." It wasn't really a question, and she sort of winked at me.

Venus may have been a total airhead, but she wasn't stupid.

"Yeah," I said, suddenly fascinated by the door jamb.

"Come on inside." She called upstairs, "Wade!" Then she looked at me again and asked like she really gave a damn, "How you doin'?"

"I'm good. I'm really good." I pulled a bag of apples out of my backpack. I'd picked it up at the supermarket on the way over—from the produce section, not the Dumpster (it had been cheap).

"What's this?"

"Hey, we're all in this together, right?"

She laughed and hugged me again. "I knew I liked you! Hey, are you hungry?" She twirled back toward the kitchen. "We were just making lunch."

"Sure." This time I hadn't even hesitated, didn't wonder where the food had come from—a Dumpster or a roadside.

Meanwhile, Wade thumped down the stairs. "Russel? What's up?" I couldn't help but notice he was wearing another crisp white t-shirt.

Venus held up the bag of apples. "He came with food!"

Wade grinned.

"I thought maybe we could hang out," I said.

He stared at me for what seemed like a long time (but for what was probably only a second). Then he smiled and said, "What do you know? Hanging out with you is exactly what I had planned for the day."

* * *

It was just Wade, Venus, and me for lunch. Venus served mussels and crab gathered from a local beach and (of course) a generous mound of seaweed. Even knowing all I knew about the freegans, they could still shock me with every new meal.

"It's a little slimy," Venus said, meaning the seaweed. "But it's so good for you! And it's the most sustainable food on Earth. Even more than insects!"

"Insects?" I said.

"Insects are the best kind of animal protein there is," Venus said, completely serious. "It takes ten pounds of plant feed to make one pound of animal meat. But with insects, ten pounds of feed makes nine pounds of meat."

"Insect meat," I said.

"Yeah." Her eyes were wide.

"Is that before or after you pull the little legs off?"

"You're making fun of me," Venus said. "But it's true. Lots of cultures already eat insects—grubs and worms too."

"Oh, well, you didn't say anything about grubs and worms," I said. "That's totally different."

"You're still making fun of me," Venus said. She thought for a second, then gave me a big smile. "But I like you anyway!"

Wade cleared his throat. "I know we freegans need to work on our P.R.," he said. "But the fact is she's right. It's all just a question of perspective. You know, lobsters are carrion feeders—they eat all the rotting stuff on the ocean floor. The idea of eating a lobster used to be considered totally disgusting. Now they're the world's most prized delicacy. Perspectives change."

"I didn't know that about lobster," I said. I thought for a second, then said, deadpan, "It still doesn't make me want to eat grubs and insects."

Wade laughed. "How about we go for a walk?" We were mostly done with lunch now.

"Where to?" I said.

He hesitated again, then a mysterious smile slipped onto his face. "You'll see." Clearly, this was something else he couldn't tell me, but could only show me.

This time, we left our bikes behind and set out on foot, through alleys and down side roads. Not far from the house, we came to a big, flat field thick with scotch broom. The plants were fat and wide, and yet also somehow spindly. They hadn't bloomed yet, and their spiky, dark green branches stuck straight up in the air, swaying in the breeze like the flailing, hairy legs of giant overturned insects (Venus and the freegans would eat for years!).

We set out down a trail, and before long, we'd been engulfed by the scratchy plants. I couldn't see the road behind us—couldn't even hear the sound of passing cars, and it had been a pretty busy street. I was surprised to see that the ground was made of rock.

No, not rock, I realized: concrete. But it was so old that it was crumbling away, had already cracked into chunks. Weeds grew from the cracks, prying them more open still. I'd always wondered about that—how a simple little weed could break through concrete.

"It was an airport," Wade explained. "A long time ago. This was the runway."

I looked around. I could see it now. It was so obvious I couldn't believe I hadn't seen it before: how flat everything was, and the long stretch of concrete that peeked out through the scotch broom in front of us. There were even a few chipped and faded lines of yellow or white paint that must have once guided the planes. But if there'd been any buildings—hangars or ticket counters—they had long ago surrendered to the weeds and scotch broom.

Wade and I walked side-by-side down that runway, and it was hard not to think about a world a hundred or a thousand years in the future, after nuclear war or global warming, after civilization had fallen and all that remained were the traces of our former cities.

"It's spooky," I said. "I can see why you wanted to show it to me."

"Oh, this isn't what I wanted to show you," he said. "We're not there yet."

The runway ran straight into a greenbelt, and another trail wound off through the trees—a strip of stubborn forest pushed back behind hills and deep into narrow canyons. We followed this new trail, the sun shining down through emerald leaves. A couple of times we passed homeless people—once I saw another cluster of tents and tarps through the undergrowth. As usual, Wade waved and called out to people. He knew almost everyone by name.

We passed the opening to a tunnel in a hillside—a big concrete culvert of some sort that was completely covered with graffiti. The city had blocked the opening with an iron grate, but someone had peeled open some of the bars, allowing access inside. Is this what Wade had wanted to show me?

But he didn't stop. "Don't go in there," he said under his breath. "Some scary folk live in there."

At first I wasn't sure if he was kidding, but his face was deadly serious. I wanted to ask him more when I saw someone on the trail in front of us. Wade said, "Matthew!" It was one of the other freegans from Wade's house, the guy with the literally dirty blond hair (not so dirty now).

For a second, he looked surprised to see us. Then he smiled and said, "Hey, Wade. And Russel." It was so strange that the freegans all knew and remembered my name. I've been going to school with some of the same people since kindergarten, and I'm pretty sure more than a few of them couldn't pick me out of a police line-up.

"What's up?" Wade said.

Matthew shrugged, almost nervously, and his

frayed backpack rustled. "Hunting and gathering. The usual."

"See if you have anything for George," Wade said, nodding back toward the homeless camp we'd passed before. "I'm still worried he's not eating."

Matthew nodded, and Wade and I walked on.

I thought about the greenbelt we were in now and the one we'd explored before, and also the vacant lots and abandoned rail tracks that Wade and I had passed through earlier in the week. In a way, the freegans had their own roads. And maybe it wasn't just roads: it was almost like there was a whole shadow city right alongside the other one. And it was populated by real people—the homeless and the freegans and whoever lived inside the graffiti-covered tunnel that Wade had warned me about. Isn't that what Wade had told me before, that freegans knew a city's secret things—its hidden people and places?

Sure, you could argue that "our" city was a lot better—that we had paved, well-lit roads and hot showers. And we definitely had a lot of "things." But I was starting to see Wade's point about how sometimes things were just a way to distract yourself, to avoid seeing the world as it is. For most teenagers, "hanging out" pretty much means playing video games, eating fast food, or going to the mall. But you couldn't do any of those things if you didn't have any money. Instead, the freegans actually went out into the world and interacted with it—the non-shopping mall world, I mean.

They made real choices. They didn't just do what the television told them to do—in fact, they did the exact opposite.

It was all so confusing. I couldn't imagine anyone more ridiculed and disrespected than the freegans: they were the Brian Bunds of the non-high school world. And yet here they were doing all these interesting, even noble things, things that most parents would *kill* to have their teenagers do. So why all the disrespect? Why was it acceptable to volunteer at a soup kitchen or go for a hike in the woods, but not acceptable to actually know homeless people by name or explore the abandoned airport near your house?

Had Venus been right? Did being a freegan really mean being free?

Wade and I were walking alongside a golf course now—a field of rolling grass. On the other side of a chain link fence, the sprawling clubhouse complex loomed.

I stopped and took it all in.

"That's pretty," I said, meaning the vivid green grass.

Wade didn't say anything.

"What?" I said, looking over at him.

"Nothing. I just feel like I've been doing nothing but lecturing you for the past two weeks."

I laughed. "It's okay. You have interesting things to say. Besides, you haven't been lectured to until you've been friends with Min."

Now Wade laughed. Then he said, "Well, golf courses are frustrating because they look so green and pretty, but they're horrible for the environment. Most of the courses use massive amounts of chemicals—to get the grass green and kill the weeds. And even if some courses are getting better, they still use so much water." He waved at the hill behind us. "This golf course even has its own water tower." Sure enough, there was a big pale green cylinder rising out of the trees on top. "And because they use so much water, all the chemicals get washed right into the streams and rivers."

I stared out at the grass. I hadn't known what Wade was telling me. But he was right about it being deceptive, because it looked so pretty.

A head popped up right in front of us.

Wade and I both jumped back.

It was a boy, maybe ten years old. His clothes were filthy, and there were dirt smudges on his face—dirt that was almost too perfect, like it was make-up on the orphans in a stage production of *Les Misérables*. His shoes were duct-taped together.

"Ha!" the boy said, pleased he'd scared us. He had been hiding in a tunnel that must have passed under the trail—like the culvert from before, but smaller.

"Andy?" Wade said to the boy. "What are you doing down there?"

"This is where we live now," he said proudly.

"Is Molly with you?"

146

The boy nodded as an older woman stood up next to him. She wasn't any better-dressed—or cleaner— than the boy. But unlike the kid, she was ducking down behind the concrete, fearful. For a second, I wondered if she was afraid of whoever Wade had warned me about earlier. Then I realized she was pretty much just nuts.

"Andy, get down!" she said, already pulling him back into the tunnel.

"Molly, you know you're always welcome at our house, right?" Wade called after her.

When she didn't answer, Wade and I walked on. We weren't talking now. Truthfully, I was annoyed by Molly. She clearly had mental problems. And what about Wade? Was there no room in his world-view for Child Protective Services?

A few minutes later, he stopped in the middle of the trail, glancing in both directions.

"What?" I said.

"I want to show you something," he said. "Remember?"

"Oh. Yeah." I really had forgotten.

"But I don't think anyone knows about it but me—I only found it by accident. I want to leave it that way, so I want to make sure we're alone."

I didn't say anything, just let him lead me off the trail right into the bushes, which were especially thick here. They weren't dark and spiky like the scotch broom back at the abandoned airport. No, under the cover of the trees, these plants were lush and soft and green, but also easily torn.

We fumbled down an unexpectedly steep slope, then forged our way forward through the undergrowth. For a minute, I thought Wade was lost.

Then he peeled back some more branches to reveal a little clearing. And in the middle was something that definitely wasn't part of the forest—and yet it was. Or, rather, it was something man-made, but it was now almost completely covered with vines.

It looked like a small bus. I think it had once been painted red with yellow trim, but the colors had long since faded. Now it was mostly the color of the forest—the green vines that covered it, that held it upright like the fingers of a giant hand.

"What is it?" I said.

"An abandoned streetcar. From the 1940s, I think."

Once he said that, I immediately saw it—the driver's seat at either end, the rusted rail wheels mostly buried in the ground. And it seemed Wade was right about no one else knowing it was here: it wasn't covered with graffiti like the culvert had been. Most of the windows were even still intact.

But how was that possible? How could it have been here all these years and no one except Wade had discovered it? Did it mean that there was a little patch of woods right here in the middle of the city that, because of some quirk of geography, no one except

Wade had seen in almost eighty years? Or *had* other people come here—a few of them, over the years—but they'd somehow also seen the beauty of this little clearing, and they'd left it alone? I wasn't sure which was more unlikely.

That's when I realized: it wasn't just people who were surprising me lately. The city was too. It was just like Wade had said—there were hidden things all around me, but I'd never really taken the time to notice. All it took was a willingness to wander a few dozen yards from the road most traveled—even the road most traveled only by freegans!

Wade walked up to the doors. They were open, and he stepped inside. I half expected the whole thing to collapse, but it had already sunk as far into the earth as it was going to. It didn't budge.

I followed Wade inside. The streetcar was solid against the ground, but I hadn't noticed from the outside how lop-sided it was, how it listed to one side. Even so, the roof and windows were more or less intact, so except for the area right by the door, the interior was surprisingly well-preserved. Even the wooden seats, covered with some kind of thick varnish, weren't decaying at all. I expected the inside to smell musty, but it didn't. It was just like the rest of the forest, like something fresh and alive.

It felt like stepping into another world, like going back in time. The white light fixtures along the ceiling were all intact, like they might flicker to life at any moment. Advertising panels had once lined the roof, but the ink on most of the cardboard had long since faded. I could make out two vague words: "unspoken passion."

"There used to be a whole network of streetcars," Wade said. "Even in a city as small as ours. You could get anywhere you wanted—even all the way out to Randall Lake—and you didn't need a car. But in the 1940s, the tire and car companies bought the streetcar companies and put them out of business. They did the same thing all over the country. People didn't know. Everyone in America thinks they're so free, thinks they can do whatever they want—that they have all these choices. But they don't have any idea how manipulated they are. How corporations force them to do exactly what they want and then convince them that was really what they wanted all along."

"I didn't know that," I said. Like with Min, being with Wade reminded me just how little I really knew.

Wade walked to the far end of the car, then fiddled with one of the brass poles that hung above the seats—hand-rails for those who had been forced to stand. He didn't say anything for a second. Then he said, quietly, "It's hard."

"What is?" I said.

"Feeling so different from everyone else."

I froze, both excited and scared. Was Wade finally telling me his own unspoken passion? But I was determined not to jump to any conclusions. So I said,

"Well, at least you have the other freegans."

He shrugged. "Sometimes I'm not even sure I fit in with them."

"Yeah?" I said, the excitement and fear rising in equal proportions.

"What does it mean that I even feel different from people who are different? You know? I don't even fit in with the freaks."

I snorted. "I know exactly what you mean. They have their own haircuts, their own fashion. But I don't care about any of that. I don't even think that's that different, you know? I think that's more about rebellion. Which is fine, I guess. But so often it just seems like a big, pointless 'fuck you' directed out at the world. It's still letting other people define you. It's not about you defining yourself."

Wade turned around to face me, both of us standing at opposite ends of the streetcar. He was in the middle of the aisle, leaning to one side along with the car. But I was in the aisle leaning to one side too, so he and the rest of the streetcar seemed normal. It was the world outside the car that was askew.

"That's it exactly," Wade said. "I knew you'd understand."

I *did* understand! I totally understood! Assuming he was also talking about being gay. Which he was, right? I mean, this was more than just the feeling he didn't quite fit in around the other freegans—it had to be. A straight guy didn't bring another guy to his cool, secret street-car-in-the-woods, right? He was gay and into me. Validate my reality here! (I keep asking you to, but you never do.)

"So," I said. "I'm curious."

"Hmm?"

"You said you were thinking about leaving town. Moving to the big city. Are you still thinking that?"

He picked at the wainscoting. "I don't know," he said, almost a whisper. "Maybe. Maybe not."

Now what did *that* mean? The only reason he would have changed his plans was because of me, right? I was his unspoken passion, right? There was no other possible way to interpret all this!

So why was he still hesitating?

Suddenly, I knew: Wade hadn't come out yet. He hadn't spoken his unspoken passion to anyone else, maybe not even himself. This was all new to him. I was scared he might reject me, but he was scared of something far more terrifying: saying the words "I'm gay" out loud for the very first time. That's why he kept showing me things he'd never shown anyone before—his belongings, this streetcar. He was working his way up to showing me a secret part of himself. Why hadn't I realized all this before?

"Wade," I said. "I need to tell you something."

He didn't say anything, just looked over at me. We were still both on opposite ends of the streetcar.

For a second, I just shuffled my feet. How did you come out and just ask someone if they were gay? Unspoken passions were unspoken for a reason.

"I like you," I said at last. "As more than a friend."

Wade didn't say anything, just stared down at the floorboards.

"And," I said, "I think you like me too, but I'm still not sure."

He didn't look up. No floorboards anywhere in the whole world had ever been as interesting as the ones Wade was looking at now.

"So I wanted to ask," I said. "Do you?"

But all this fighting against the outside world was suddenly too much for him. He grabbed onto one of the brass beams for support.

Wade looked up at last. "Yes," he said evenly. "I like you. As more than a friend."

I grinned. Wade's unspoken passions had been spoken at last! There really was a reason for all those clean t-shirts! My reality had been validated!

So what did I do now? I had a feeling Wade had never kissed a guy before: it was something about how hesitant he was. So did he want me to kiss him now?

I took a step toward him. It seemed like the floor shifted despite the streetcar being set so firmly in the mud. Or maybe it was just my foot sliding on the angled floor.

Wade started walking toward me—his feet slipped a little too—but we met pretty much in the middle.

"Can I kiss you?" I said. As soon as I said this, I remembered this was almost exactly what Kevin had said to me almost a year earlier, at the same park where I'd later caught him hooking up with a guy. I'd been so nervous back then, but I wasn't nervous now. On the contrary, it felt exciting to be the experienced one for a change, to be the one in charge, especially since Wade was two years older than me.

"Yeah," he breathed. "You can."

So I did. His lips were firmer than Kevin's or Otto's. I slipped my tongue into his mouth. He still smelled like salt and pine—no blackberry now—but he tasted sweeter than that, like honey, with a touch of something bitter, like coffee.

Boy, had my reality been validated!

Underneath the kiss, I felt him smile. It's a great feeling, kissing a smile.

"What?" I said.

"It's just not what I thought it would feel like." So I'd been right: he'd never been with a guy before.

"Is that good?" I said.

Just inches from my face, he nodded. "It's good."

Then we kissed again, and I was hugging him. His body was different from Kevin's and Otto's too— thicker. He hugged me back—tentatively, awkwardly.

"Your skin," I said. "It's not really black. It's like chestnut reflected in copper. I see all kinds of different colors—black and brown and yellow and orange."

He blushed exactly the way I'd blushed when Kevin had complimented my hair and my eyes that night in the park. I hadn't even known that black people could blush, but now I knew they did. It was just really, really subtle, like the faintest glimmer of a red dawn.

I smiled and kissed him again. A weed had broken through the concrete of my heart. (Yes, I know that's over-the-top. Go with it.)

"I know this is new to you," I said. "We can take it slow." He nodded, and we took a seat in that streetcar. Because of the slope, I found myself sliding toward him, my hip pushing against his. "Can I ask you a personal question?" I said.

"It'd be stupid of me to say no now."

"Is this part of the reason why you became a freegan?" I specifically didn't say "gay," because I didn't know for sure what Wade was. Maybe he was bisexual. Or "questioning."

He leaned back in the seat. This window was completely covered with vines on the outside—I couldn't see out.

"No," he said. "But I think it's a little *like* being a freegan. Wanting something, but not being quite sure what it is. Not being able to put it into words. And then finally experiencing it and realizing what it was you were missing all along."

I nodded.

And yet, something was different from that night when I'd been with Kevin. Wade was still hesitating. With Kevin, I'd been nervous, but I hadn't hesitated.

"What is it?" I asked.

He sat forward in his seat, elbows on the top of

the seat in front of us—closed, protected. "Truthfully, this *is* all pretty new to me. It's going to take some time to process. Is that okay?"

"Are you kidding?" I said. "Of course it's okay! Hey, I need to process it too." The truth is there were all kinds of different ways of being gay or bisexual. I'd been putting it into words long before I'd even met Kevin, at least to myself. But maybe not every guy did. It didn't feel like Wade had.

"But Russel?" he said. "You need to know something."

"Okay."

"One of these days, I am leaving to go to the city. Not right away, not if anything happens between us. But eventually. I have to. I *want* to. I want to get away from my family. But I also want to make a difference."

On one hand, this disappointed me. On the other hand, it was exactly the kind of thing that attracted me to Wade in the first place.

"But..." he said.

But?

"There's no reason why you couldn't come with me."

Was Wade serious? Was he really asking me if I wanted to join the freegans? But I could see in his deep brown eyes that he was.

There actually *was* a reason I couldn't go with Wade, a good one: I was only seventeen years old. If I left now, I'd be "running away from home" and the whole fricking world would end. But I wouldn't be seventeen years old forever. In less than a year, I'd be an adult.

Could I see myself joining the freegans then? My parents' heads would definitely explode. Going to Europe for a year before college was one thing, but becoming a freegan? Then again, I thought about all the interesting things I'd seen and experienced since I'd met Wade—things right here in the town that I'd thought was so incredibly boring before. What would it be like to live this way all the time?

"Maybe," I said to Wade. "At least for a little while." Even as I said this, I remembered how Wade had only meant to join the freegans for a few months and had ended up staying for a year and a half.

That said, I'd said I wanted adventure.

Boy, had I found it.

When I got home that night, I knew I'd never be able to sleep, not as excited as I was. Part of me wanted to call or IM Min or Gunnar to tell them what had happened, but I'd been keeping Wade a secret from them for so long now that another part of me wanted to go on doing it.

So as usual, I IMed Otto instead.

OttoManEmpire: So what happened? I want DETAILS!

So I gave him details—all about the walk in the woods and the hidden streetcar. But I'm going to tell you what I told Otto: nothing did "happen," except for a bit more kissing. I wanted to respect Wade's choice on that. Besides—hey!—what makes you think that I'm such a slut that I'm willing to drop my pants at the first sign of someone being interested in me? I wanted to move slowly too.

But here's the weird part: I didn't tell Otto how Wade had asked me if I could ever see myself becoming a freegan, and that I'd said I could. What was *that* about? Maybe freeganism really *was* a cult, and I just couldn't see it. I mean, if I really had been brainwashed, I wouldn't know it, right?

OttoManEmpire: Oh, man, that sounds so romantic.

Smuggler: It was. It really, really was.

It was at that point I finally remembered who I was talking to, that I'd once shared romantic nights with Otto too—that he and I had once been boyfriends.

Smuggler: I hope I'm not depressing you. You'll meet someone too, you know.

OttoManEmpire: Well...

Smuggler: Well what?

OttoManEmpire: Well, maybe I already have.

Smuggler: WHAT?!!?! Tell me, tell me, tell me!!! Tell me EVERYTHING!

Otto had a new boyfriend too! It was the guy he'd been interested in all along—someone he knew from student council. And deep into the night, Otto told me all about him.

CHAPTER TWELVE

The next day, Sunday, I rode back to Wade's. But halfway there, I passed a gas station at a busy intersection, and I saw Leah standing at one of the pumps. She was wearing military fatigues, and it looked like she was just finishing up filling her car.

Was Min with her? There was definitely someone inside the car waiting. Still, Leah went to a different school, and I knew she had a whole life apart from Min. Even so, I wanted to say hi, so I veered into the parking lot on my bike. I reminded myself not to mention Min's birthday or the surprise party—I didn't even want to begin to explain how I knew she was planning a party.

Leah still hadn't seen me. She'd walked around to the front of her car and was getting back inside.

"Leah!" I called, but she didn't hear me over the noisy intersection. Inside the car, she closed the door and leaned over to kiss the person sitting next to her. I saw it all perfectly from behind. It wasn't a little kiss either.

So it was Min after all. Right? Because it had to be. Didn't it? After what we'd seen in Leah's bedroom? How stupid Min had felt?

Leah pulled forward and turned to the right. But now I could see the person sitting next to her in the car. I didn't necessarily *want* to see—a big part of me just wanted to keep on riding, not even looking back. I wanted to forget I'd ever seen Leah.

But it was too late. I'd seen the person in the car with Leah, and it wasn't Min. It was some guy. Why would Leah be planning a birthday party for Min even though she was dating someone else?

I didn't know. But now I did know that for all of Min's seemingly paranoid suspicions and her crazy plot to break into Leah's house, she had been right: Leah really was cheating on her.

And somehow I had to break it to her.

I rode straight over to Min's. I texted her to say I was stopping by, but that's all. I figured this was something I needed to say in person.

Min's mom let me inside, and I found Min on the computer in her bedroom. "I have something to tell you," I said, "but you have to promise me you won't freak out."

"I'm freaking out just by your making me promise not to freak out," she said.

"I just ran into Leah at a gas station. She didn't see me. She was kissing a guy."

Min didn't say anything. Her aquarium gurgled.

I wasn't sure how long to wait for Min to react. But finally, I said, "You were right. She's cheating on you."

She inhaled at last. "Who is it?"

"I don't know, but I took a picture." As they'd waited to pull out into traffic on the other side of the gas station, I'd taken a picture with my phone. It was blurry, and Leah and the guy obviously weren't kissing anymore. But it was clearly Leah's car.

"Well?" I said.

"I can't make him out. They were really kissing?"

I nodded. "And not like a little peck either. What are you going to do?"

Truthfully, I kind of expected her to say that she wanted my help to break into Leah's house again, or maybe steal her phone to read her text messages. But instead, she turned to me in her chair and said, "What choice do I have? I need to talk to her."

That Monday, I was hurrying between classes. I had Calculus in the far end of one building and American Literature in a classroom that was pretty much on the exact opposite side of campus, and I only had five

162

minutes to get between them. I almost never actually made it on time—the laws of physics were not my friend—but it seemed to be enough for the teacher if I managed to show up in the thirty-second grace period after the last bell, at least if I was sweaty and out of breath.

Halfway there—across a plaza, and through the visitor parking lot, and up two outside staircases—I heard an angry voice from up ahead.

"Screw you, Land! I thought you were my friend!"

"Well," another voice said, "that was your first mistake."

Kevin.

I stepped out into a little courtyard between buildings. Kevin stood off to one side with his friend Ben. Kevin's back was to me, but Ben was getting right up in his face.

I slowed. I was desperate to get to class, but let's face it: I was also curious to know what this little interaction was about. American Literature waited for no man, it's true, but it was admittedly a little more lenient on an A student like me. And for the time being, the three of us were basically alone in that courtyard.

"I just don't get it," Ben said. "Why would you tell all those lies about me?"

"Who says they were lies?" Kevin said.

"Jesus, you're a dick! How come I never saw what a dick you are before?"

What was this? Now Kevin was telling lies about

his friend Ben?

"Don't talk to me!" Ben said, his finger back in Kevin's face. "Not ever again! And if I hear that you're telling lies about me ever again, I'll knock your fucking head off!"

"I am *so* scared," Kevin said, sagging like a bucket seat.

Even so, it sounded like this little talk of theirs was winding up, so that was my cue to hurry along the courtyard again. Ben and Kevin had never even noticed me.

But as I walked on, I thought: Ha! I knew it! I'd known all along what a raging asshole Kevin is. Now I had proof. Why in the world had I ever even doubted it? I might have been peeking at him all these months, but I really never had *seen* him. He and Brian probably weren't even friends—Brian had probably just been tutoring him.

I had no idea if I was going to end up a freegan or not, but I now knew for sure I was meant to be with Wade, not Kevin.

That afternoon after school, Min told me she still hadn't talked to Leah, but that she was going to go confront her in person.

"Will you come with me?" she asked.

"Where?" I said, confused. "When?"

"To her house. Now."

Truthfully, this was the last thing I wanted to do. I'd been planning to ride over and see Wade again—I hadn't seen him since Saturday. But it sounded like Min needed me, and I didn't want to make her invoke the "friend" bat-signal again, so I nodded.

"But what's the plan exactly?" I said.

"I'm not sure. I guess I'll know when we get there."

So I told Gunnar to ride home without me, then I threw my bike in the back of Min's car, and she drove us over to the non-existent Cranberry Creek. This time, we got beeped in through the front gate.

Leah answered her front door. "Hey, Russel." She clearly hadn't expected me to be with Min.

"Hey," I mumbled.

"Well, come on in. What's up?" She led us into the foyer, which had a high ceiling and a fancy chandelier.

Min hesitated by a vase full of pussy willows, and I expected her to say something, but she didn't, just looked sort of tongue-tied. So far, she hadn't said anything at all.

Finally, I said to Leah, "We need to talk."

"Talk?" Leah said, confused, looking from me to Min. "About what?"

"Is there somewhere we can go?" I said, knowing full well how weird this was, that I was the one saying the things Min was supposed to say.

"Sure. Let's go out to the pool."

So we did. It was also weird having been here once

before, seeing the pool area from a different angle. Leah's parents were gone, and I was glad—the last thing I wanted was to run into Leah's lecherous dad. It was cold outside, but Leah turned on this heat lamp as we sat at a table by the pool. It smelled like chlorine and wet compost from a garden bed. Somewhere nearby, a water pump whined.

"Do you guys want something to drink?" Leah said.

"I know you're seeing someone," Min said out of the blue.

Leah didn't say anything for a second, just once again looked between Min and me. Even now, I was forty percent sure this had all been some kind of massive misunderstanding—that the guy I'd seen Leah with was her closeted gay best friend trying to prove to the rest of the school he was straight.

But then Leah looked out over the pool and sort of slumped in her seat. The legs of her chair scraped against the concrete.

"What?" Min said.

"Can we talk about this alone?" Leah said, meaning me.

"No," Min said. "I want Russel here. I want him to hear."

"How did you find out?" Leah said.

So it was true? Leah really *was* cheating on Min? Like father, like daughter, I guess. Did everyone lie? First Kevin, now Leah.

"A *guy*?" Min said. I don't know why she sounded so outraged. Min was bisexual after all.

"What makes you think it's a guy?" Leah said. She sounded truly mystified.

"I saw you with him," I said. "At a gas station. Kissing."

Leah considered for a second, then shook her head. "No. It's a girl. She's just butch."

Min looked at me. Could the cute guy I'd seen Leah with have been a girl? I shrugged.

"Min, I'm so sorry," Leah said. "I didn't want to hurt you." She reached forward to take Min's hand, and the bottom of her chair scraped the concrete again.

But Min pulled her hand away before they touched. "You didn't want to *hurt* me? Are you kidding?"

"No." Leah shook her head. "I'm sorry, that was a stupid thing to say. I'm just really sorry about everything. It hasn't felt right for a while now, but I didn't know how to tell you."

"You didn't know how to tell me," Min repeated. She sounded almost dead, like a zombie. I felt a little zombie-like myself, and I was only the one who had seen Leah with the other girl.

"Min, I'm *so* sorry!" Leah said. She was starting to cry.

Min stood up. Her eyes were bone dry. "Let's go, Russel."

I stood up too and together we walked toward the front door. I noticed a single pussy willow on the ceramic tile in the foyer.

From behind, Leah said, "You're not going to tell anyone about us, are you?" Even now, she was worried about being outed, about her friends finding out she was a lesbian. That pissed *me* off, because I knew that was the last thing in the world Min would ever do. How could anyone who once claimed to love Min think that was even an option?

Min didn't say a word, and she definitely didn't look back at Leah. She just inhaled, straightened her back, and walked out through the front door.

We'd traveled here in Min's car, but I offered to drive her home and she let me. She stared out her side window. It wasn't until we were outside the gated community that I said, "Are you okay?"

"She's such a bitch."

"She is," I said.

She turned to look at me at last. "How did I not see it?"

"I don't know. It's not just the cheating thing. That thing she said as we were leaving, about how she thought you were going to out her to her friends. Who thinks that way?"

"I know," Min said. "I couldn't believe she said that." She sort of smiled. "It's the Elephant of Surprise."

"Boy, isn't it?" So Min also remembered that conversation we'd had at the zoo. "He always steps on you when you least expect it."

"Or she."

I smiled. "Right."

Now Min laughed. She leaned back in her seat.

"What?" I said.

"I don't know. Maybe it's like what they say about cancer—that the fear of it is actually worse than the disease. My worst fear just came true, but you know what? I don't feel that bad. It's actually sort of a relief. Which isn't to say I won't cry myself to sleep tonight, but that's then, this is now."

Her talking about how she was going to cry later made me want to cry a little too. But then Min laughed again—howled almost, which is just so not Min. Suddenly, I was seeing her express all kinds of emotion.

"What now?" I said.

"I just can't believe what shitty luck the two of us have with love!" she said.

At that, I finally let myself laugh too, even though I felt a little guilty, since it seemed like I was actually having pretty good luck with Wade.

"I know," I said. "First Kevin and Terese, then that guy Web at summer camp, then Otto and Leah. We can't win!"

Min stopped laughing.

"What?" I said.

"There's something I need to tell you about Kevin. Something important. I should've told you before, but I got so distracted by this Leah thing."

I clenched the steering wheel. "There is nothing you need to tell me about Kevin."

"No, seriously, there is!"

"Min," I said. "Seriously. I know everything I need to know." And I told her what I'd seen between Kevin and Ben earlier that day.

"Ben accused Kevin of telling lies about him?" Min said.

"Why do you sound so surprised? We knew what kind of person Kevin was."

"I don't believe it."

"Believe it. I heard it with my own ears. And last week, Gunnar saw him flipping Brian Bund shit." I definitely didn't see the need to tell her that I'd asked Gunnar to spy on him.

"But—" Min said.

"Besides, I might not be so unlucky in love after all."

"What are you talking about?"

Before I could say anything more, my phone rang. I could see it was Gunnar.

"Would you get that?" I said to Min, and she did.

They talked for a second. Min listened and then said, "Are you serious?"

Gunnar said something else over the phone.

"Okay, okay, we will," Min said, and hung up. She

didn't say anything to me right away. Now she was back to staring out the side window.

"*What?*" I said, dying to know what that had been all about.

"We need to go see Gunnar. Right away."

"Why?"

"He's been going over some of the photos he's been taking. And he's convinced that Wade and the freegans are terrorists and are planning to blow something up."

CHAPTER THIRTEEN

"This is *crazy*," I said to Gunnar. Min and I had driven straight over to his house and he'd taken us to his room. "The freegans aren't terrorists!"

"Maybe they are, maybe they aren't," Gunnar said. "Just let me show you what I found, okay?"

Before I go on, I suppose I need to describe Gunnar's bedroom the way I described mine and Min's, but honestly, I'm not sure I have the time. Yes, it's just as weird as you'd think and yes, the shrunken heads are real, but they're probably just monkeys.

Gunnar had a bunch of screen-shots queued up on his computer. First, he showed us the freegan front room. I'd forgotten how dirty and messy it was. Mostly when I thought of the freegans, I thought of Wade who wasn't dirty at all.

"So?" I said.

"So the first thing I noticed was these papers on the floor," Gunnar said. "I don't know why they caught my eye, but they did." He pointed to the papers with the cartoon elf.

"I remember," I said. "I figured they must have had a kid stay there at some point." I pointed to the copy of *Curious George* on the floor. "See?"

"No," Gunnar said. "The papers are something different. I think it's a newsletter. The cartoon elf is some kind of logo or graphic. Can you make out the word at the top?"

Min squinted. "'Elf,'" she said.

"So the freegans are actually a secret community of elves?" I said. I admit I was being a bit of a butt here. Part of it was that I had all kinds of things on my mind, and I just wasn't interested in humoring another one of Gunnar's endless obsessions right then. But maybe another part of it was all those lingering suspicions I'd had about the freegans right from the beginning. I guess I didn't want to hear that they may have been right, especially not now that I'd fallen so head-over-heels for Wade.

"'E.L.F.,'" Gunnar said. "In all caps." He showed us a zoomed-in version of the screen-cap. "It's an acronym. It stands for Earth Liberation Front. They're a radical environmental group. They believe in eco-terrorism."

"Oh, God, no!" Min said. "I've heard about these people. Total idiots. They say that environmental issues are too urgent to wait for political change, that they have to stop polluters by any means necessary."

Gunnar nodded. "Anything short of hurting people."

"They also say that by being so extreme, they make other environmental activists look moderate," Min said, still fuming. "But that's either stupid or naive. All they're really doing is making it incredibly easy to paint *all* environmentalists as dangerous extremists. And that makes it even harder to get anyone to care about the environment."

"So someone at the freegan house was reading something from E.L.F.," I said. "So what? That doesn't mean they're members of E.L.F. People come and go there. Maybe an E.L.F. member stayed there once. You saw the photographs of all the people on their bulletin board."

"Exactly right," Gunnar said. "And that bulletin board is exactly what I wanted to show you next." Sure enough, he showed us a picture of the bulletin board with the snapshots of all the people who had stayed in the house.

"What about it?" I said. Everyone looked perfectly normal to me. Well, perfectly normal for freegans.

Gunnar pointed to the wrench sitting on top of the frame.

"It's a wrench," I said. "I remember seeing it when we were there."

"Specifically, it's a monkey wrench," Gunnar said.

"So?" I said again. "Everyone has a monkey wrench."

"That's true. But it's kind of a weird place to keep a wrench, don't you think? It's almost like it's a symbol or something, or a secret code. And the thing is, a monkey wrench also happens to be another symbol for E.L.F. They say they're against killing people, and it's true no one has ever directly died from any of their actions. Well, that's debatable. But they definitely believe in mucking things up—throwing a wrench into the workings of industries that pollute, logging companies, things like that. So the monkey wrench is a pretty good symbol for what they stand for."

"This is all very interesting," I said. "But it could all be a complete coincidence. People do that all the time—they see connections that aren't there. Min, what's the word for that?"

"Apophenia," she said. "The human tendency to see patterns in random data."

"Yes!" I said. "Or maybe some of the freegans *do* sort of sympathize with the Earth Liberation Front. I mean, we know they're pretty radical people. They eat out of Dumpsters, remember? None of this proves anything. It definitely doesn't mean they're *terrorists*."

"Or pareidolia," Min said. "That's the phenomenon in which people see or hear identifiable images or sounds that don't really exist. Like when people see the face of Jesus in a piece of toast."

"Okay, Min," I said. "Give it a rest."

"I'm not done," Gunnar said, which, frankly, was exactly what I was afraid he was going to say. "Remember when Wade showed us the freegan store?"

"Of course I remember!" I said. "It was only two weekends ago." But even as I said this, I thought: had I really only known Wade for less than two weeks?

Gunnar showed us a photograph he'd taken of the freegan store. "Look at the shelves on the back wall," he said, zooming in.

They looked exactly like I remembered them.

I turned to Gunnar, confused.

He pointed to a wooden crate at the very bottom of the shelving, then zoomed in even closer.

The words "Fire Ant Explosives" were clearly written in red paint.

Suddenly, I had a very bad feeling about this.

Down below, in even smaller letters, it said, "Dynamite." When we'd actually been there, I'd thought this had been a box of fireworks, but it wasn't.

The freegans kept sticks of dynamite in their store? I know they encouraged people to contribute whatever they could, but dynamite? That was ridiculous.

Even so, I said, "There are legitimate reasons to have dynamite. Or maybe that's left over from whoever used the garage before."

Gunnar just stared at me, didn't say a word.

Meanwhile, Min kept squinting at the photo.

I was afraid to ask her what she'd spotted, but I knew I had to. "What is it?" I said.

She pointed to the photo, to something next to the dynamite on those shelves. "Here. This tool."

I squinted too. "Hedge clippers?"

"It's not hedge clippers," Min said. "It's a bolt-cutter."

"No..."

"Russel, yes. And bolt-cutters aren't just used for cutting bolts. They also cut—"

"Locks." Gunnar nodded. "That was my last piece of evidence. I was trying to make it as dramatic as possible, to sort of build tension. Did it work?"

Min ignored him as usual. "I wonder what they're planning," she said.

"Oh!" Gunnar said. "There *is* one more piece of evidence—I forgot. After I found all this, I searched the local newspaper for stories involving dynamite." He pulled up an article on the computer screen. "Two weeks ago, someone tried to blow up a tractor at a new housing development. Police thought it was vandals, but I think it was eco-terrorists."

Min sat back in her chair with a gesture that said, Well, I'm totally convinced.

But I wasn't, not at all.

"This is stupid!" I said. "Wade would never be involved in anything like that!"

Both Min and Gunnar looked at me. I guess I'd spoken more loudly than I'd intended. I was also clenching my fists.

Finally, Min asked, very gently, "How do you

know?"

"What?" I said.

"You just sound pretty convinced. Why are you so certain? What, have you been dating Wade or something?"

"No. Maybe. Yes."

"*What?*" Min said. My words had set off a detonation on her face. "And you didn't *tell* me? For how long?"

Meanwhile, Gunnar just sort of smiled to himself.

"It's complicated," I said. "We've been sort of seeing each other, but it really only got romantic this past weekend. But the point is I *know* Wade. He's not that kind of person. I know for a fact he wouldn't be involved in anything like this. This is all just pointless speculation."

"Are you absolutely, positively sure?" Min said. "Because people's lives could be at stake here."

"Yes, I'm absolutely, positively—" But right then I remembered something Wade had told me.

I'll do what I have to do to change the world, he'd said. *Whatever it takes—anything at all.*

I didn't see how blowing something up was going to make people any more likely to listen to the freegan point-of-view. It would do the exact opposite, just like Min had said. On the other hand, it definitely sounded like something a member of E.L.F. might *think* would help change the world. Wade had even talked about a "revolution" coming. Had he meant an armed revolution?

Then I remembered something else he'd told me:
We'll probably all be moving on soon anyway.

"What?" Min said.

I repeated everything Wade had told me.

Min bolted up from the computer. "We need to call the police."

"No," I said.

Min and Gunnar looked at me.

"I still don't believe it," I said. "I *can't* believe it. You don't know Wade. Before we call the police, I need to talk to him."

"Russel—" Min said.

"Look, maybe this *is* just an example of apop-whatever. If we call the police and end up being wrong, we're going to ruin the lives of a whole bunch of people. Even if the freegans are totally innocent, I'm sure they'd be kicked out of that house. And do you need a permit to have dynamite? And who knows what other stuff might be there—drugs or whatever? They could go to jail, all because we couldn't even be bothered to ask for an explanation. That's just wrong."

Min thought for a second. "But if *you're* wrong, people's lives could be in danger."

I nodded. "So give me fifteen minutes. We'll go over, I'll talk to Wade. If the freegans really are eco-terrorists, what are the odds they're going to strike in the next fifteen minutes?"

CHAPTER FOURTEEN

So Min, Gunnar, and I drove over to the freegan house. It was after dark by the time we got there.

"Give me ten minutes to talk to him," I said from the back seat.

Min and Gunnar looked back at me from the front seat, their two heads tipped together like a cutesy photograph.

"You really trust him that much?" Min asked me.

"I don't know," I said. "I think so.

Min and Gunnar exchanged a glance—another cutesy photograph.

Finally, Min nodded. "Okay, but I'm waiting here in the car. You guys can go in, but if I don't hear from you in exactly ten minutes, I'm calling the police."

* * *

Wade answered the door. He took one look at me and Gunnar, and said, "Russel? What is it? You look really serious."

"Can we talk for a second?" I said. "It's really important."

"Sure," he said. "Come on inside. Sit down."

I didn't move, stayed right in the entryway. The front room was empty, but I could hear laughter from the kitchen. Something bubbled on the stove. Whatever it was, it smelled horrible—sour.

Suddenly, Venus stuck her head in from the kitchen.

"Russel!" she said. "I thought I heard you. We're totally making dandelion salad with nettles tonight, and I'm totally making you some!"

I faked a smile. This was what she'd promised me all those days ago when we'd first met.

"Sure thing," I said.

When she was gone, Wade said, "What is it? What's so important?"

I looked him right in the eye and asked, "Are you a member of E.L.F.?"

Confusion flickered on his face—in his eyes and at the edges of his lips.

"No," he said.

"Do you know what E.L.F. is?" Gunnar said.

"Sure," Wade said. "It's the Environmental Liberation Front."

And with that answer, I was almost certain he was

telling the truth. If he'd been lying, he would have denied knowing what E.L.F. stood for. Wouldn't he?

"Are there any freegans who are members of E.L.F.?" Gunnar said.

"There might be," he said, suddenly wary. "We get all kinds of different people here. Once we even had a Republican. Why?"

Gunnar showed him the photos on his phone— the ones with the E.L.F. newsletters on the floor and wrench on top of the bulletin board. As Wade took in the photos, I glanced over at that bulletin board. The wrench was still there.

Inside the kitchen, voices murmured and dishes clinked. I smelled tomatoes simmering and some herb I didn't recognize. Now it didn't seem so bad. The sour smell must have been the vinegar in the salad dressing.

"Like I said, we get all kinds of people here," Wade said to Gunnar. "But that's kind of weird about the wrench. I never thought about it before."

"There's more," Gunnar said, showing him the photos from the freegan store.

At first, Wade just laughed. But when he saw from Gunnar's face that he was totally serious, his face got sober too. Once again, I was certain Wade was telling the truth about not knowing anything about eco-terrorism. If he'd been lying, his first impulse would have been to look baffled, not to laugh.

"Look," Wade said. "I agree this is really weird.

Really scary, actually. I want to get to the bottom of it. Do you mind if I ask everyone else?"

Gunnar and I exchanged a glance, and part of me was thinking: was this some kind of plan to get the others to rush us, to kidnap us, so we couldn't tell the police what we'd learned? But Min was in the car with her finger on her cell phone, and I was almost certain that Wade was telling the truth. So I nodded to him.

Wade stepped into the kitchen just as my phone vibrated. Min and I had both set our timers out in the car, and now ten minutes were up. If I didn't contact Min right now, she was going to call the police.

I texted Min, told her everything seemed okay, but to give us another five minutes.

Meanwhile, Wade was explaining to the other freegans everything Gunnar had seen in the photos. I recognized one of them, but there were two other freegans I'd never seen before.

"Hold on," I said. "Where's Venus?" She was gone.

"She said she needed something from the store out back," one of the freegans said.

"And where's Matthew?" Wade asked.

"He went with her," the freegan said, confused.

My eyes met Wade's. "They overheard us talking, and now they've gone to go do whatever they're planning. Once they're done, they're probably just going to leave town."

Sure enough, when we checked the freegan store, Venus and Matthew weren't there—and the dynamite box was open and the bolt-cutter was gone.

Gunnar, Wade, and I ran to Min, still in the car in the front yard. "Call the police!" I said. "It's Venus and Matthew. They took the dynamite and left."

"Where are they going?" Min said. "What do I tell the police?"

What *did* she tell them? What could Venus and Matthew be planning on blowing up?

"They took bikes," Wade said, "so they can't have gone far. That means wherever they're going, it's around here somewhere."

What could their target be? Somewhere on McKenzie Street? That would be pretty shitty, given how tolerant this whole neighborhood had been to the freegans. But I couldn't think of anything they might blow up there.

I remembered how the freegans had a whole system of back alleys and greenbelts that they used to travel around the city. It made sense that's what Venus and Matthew would use to get where they were going. But where was that? The garbage dump? The abandoned warehouses in the industrial district? Would anyone care if they set off dynamite in any of those places?

"The golf course," I said suddenly. "That water tower up on the hill? If they blew that up, it would flood the whole course, and probably the club house too."

I saw the glint of realization in Wade's eyes. I had to be right. Wade had made a point to tell me how bad golf courses were for the environment—the other freegans probably thought the same thing. And we'd run into Matthew in the woods near the golf course that one day. He'd even seemed sort of nervous about something.

Wade stiffened.

"What is it?" I said.

"Molly and Andy—they're living in the tunnel beneath the water tower. If they're still there when that tower blows, they'll be right in the path of the flood."

So much for the eco-terrorists not hurting people, I thought. "The police'll get there before they can do anything," I said.

"How can you be sure?" Wade said. "It's not that far on bikes, and they have a head start. There aren't any roads near that part of the greenbelt, and even if there's an access road up to the water tower, I'm sure it'll be locked, and it'll take time to get it open."

What was Wade saying? That we go after them ourselves? I was no hero. On the other hand, it was my fault that Venus and Matthew had been tipped off. I was the one who'd insisted on talking to Wade before calling the police.

So I had no choice except to say, "Let's go."

"But they took two bikes," Wade said. "We only have two left."

I turned to Gunnar and told him where to go after they called the cops—fortunately, he knew the exact area. Then Wade and I ran for the bikes.

When we reached the base of the hill with the water tower, we still hadn't seen any sign of Venus and Matthew. In other words, we didn't know if we'd come to the right place. If I'd been wrong about the target, they were going to get away with whatever they were planning, and there was nothing anyone could do about it. On the other hand, if I was right and they were planting dynamite on the water tower above us even now, it could blow at any time, and Wade and I were right in the path of where that water would rush. We'd be washed away in a raging wall of water, twisted up in our bikes and slammed into trees or maybe the fence that circled the golf course.

Could someone survive something like that?

A very narrow trail cut through the undergrowth to the top of the hill. But Wade hesitated. Still on his bike, he was staring toward the golf course, looking for the family in the bushes. "Molly? Andy?" he said quietly so as to not tip off Venus and Matthew, assuming they were even up at the water tower. "Are you there? You need to get out of here. Someone is about to blow up the water tower."

No one answered. This time, no one peeked over the edge. Had they moved on already to somewhere else? Or were they still crouched down there in hiding, and Molly was too fearful or paranoid to listen to our warnings? Even in the dark, I saw Wade thinking: was it more pressing to try and find Andy and Molly, and drag them away if possible, or was it more important to get to the top of the hill to try to stop Venus and Matthew?

I had stopped on my bike next to Wade, and I'd like to say that I hesitated for the same reason he did. But it's not true. The truth is I was frozen in fear. I couldn't stop thinking about all that water rushing down on me from above, roaring through the trees, engulfing me.

Finally, Wade made his decision: to try to stop Venus and Matthew. He started riding up the trail to the top of the hill, the wheels of his bike quietly grinding against the dirt and gravel. If I'd been alone, if Wade hadn't been in front of me shaming me into moving forward, I think I might have just turned around right there and biked off into the darkness.

But he was there, so I rolled forward after him.

In the moonlight in the clearing at the top of the hill, we saw the two other freegan bikes lying in the weeds. I'd been right: we'd come to the right place after all. And we'd made it to the water tower before they'd had a chance to blow it up. I hadn't been washed away or slammed into a tree by a raging wall of water.

The tower loomed up in front of us, a giant cylinder that I knew was painted light green, but that looked pasty white in the dark. A chain-link fence surrounded the whole thing with some surprisingly nasty-looking barbed wire on top.

Right in front of us, just a few feet from the bikes, Venus and Matthew had cut an opening in the fence, a little door in the chain-link that they'd peeled to one side so they could crawl inside.

Farther on, a couple of figures crouched in the shadow cast by the water tower. They were positioned exactly where they'd need to be if they wanted to blow open a hole in the tank in such a way that the water would rush down onto the golf course.

In frustration, I quietly squeezed the brakes on my bike.

But if Venus and Matthew were still inside the fence, that meant we still had time. I had no idea how long the timers or the fuses on dynamite were, but I knew they had to be longer than for firecrackers. Dynamite was a pretty big deal, so there had to be enough time for whoever lit it to get away. Venus and Matthew clearly thought they had enough time to light it and get outside of the chain-link fence.

I had an idea. I didn't know if it was a *good* idea—probably not—but it was the only thing I could think of on such short notice.

I whispered to Wade, "Talk to them. Try to talk

them out of what they're doing. But mostly just distract them. Don't let them know we called the police and don't tell them I'm here."

"What are you doing?" he said to me.

"You'll see," I said, pulling my bike into the shadows.

No, I wasn't fleeing in blind panic. I won't say I wasn't still *tempted* to flee in blind panic. But as Wade confronted Venus and Matthew, I quickly untied the twist-ties that kept the brakes attached to my handlebars.

"Venus, I'm *serious!*" Wade was saying. "There's a homeless family living right below us, between us and the golf course!"

"He's lying," Venus said to him. "He'll say anything to stop us."

As they talked, I crawled through the grass to the rectangular opening they'd cut in the chain-link fence. I had four twist-ties and now I was using them to seal the chain-link fence back up. I was going to trap them inside!

Over by the dynamite, Matthew stood up. "It's ready," he said. He looked over at Wade. "Get out of here. Once we light this, you're going to have exactly forty-five seconds to get out of the way."

Venus lit a match.

"I wouldn't do that," I said, now standing and

stepping out into the moonlight myself. "Not unless you want to be stuck inside there when the dynamite blows. If the explosion or the water doesn't get you, the police will. We already called them, and they're on their way."

Both Venus and Matthew looked at me, and even in the dark, even in the shadows of that water tower, I could see they didn't believe me.

"What the hell are you talking about?" Matthew said. "We cut a hole in the fence."

"Maybe you did," I said. "But I just sealed it up. You're trapped."

"We cut it *open*," Matthew said, but as he said this, he glanced over toward the little door they'd made in the fence.

It was gone. Or at least it looked like it was.

I'd been lucky that the twist-ties had been white and were now almost invisible against the light metal of the chain-link. But even if they hadn't been, I'd twisted them on really tight. I knew they could untwist them eventually, or maybe just kick their way through. They could also cut open a new hole with the bolt-cutters. But all that would take time—time they wouldn't have in the forty-five seconds they'd have once they lit the fuse on a cluster of dynamite.

The match in Venus' hand burned down to her fingers, but she didn't notice. When it burned her, she started in surprise, dropping the match, and it went out.

Somewhere nearby, maybe even at the base of the hill, sirens wailed. I smiled. If Venus and Matthew climbed or kicked their way through the fence right now, and if they were careful where they ran, they might get away. But there was no way they'd have time to fight their way through the fence *and* go back and light the dynamite, not before the police arrived.

They had to know this. My plan had worked perfectly.

"You idiot," Matthew said to me. But then he picked up the bolt-cutter lying next to him in the grass and walked over to an access door on the far side of the water tower. It was a door I hadn't even noticed. With absolutely no effort at all, he snapped the padlock with his cutter. Then he kicked the door wide open.

He looked back at Venus. "Light the dynamite," he said to her.

And she did.

CHAPTER FIFTEEN

"No!" I said, but it was too late. The fuse to the dynamite was sizzling in the darkness, and Venus and Matthew were running—out the door in the fence, away from their bikes, off into the trees.

I stared at that sparkling fuse. Wade and I had exactly forty-five seconds to get away from the water tower, or we'd be killed by a raging wall of water.

No. It was more like thirty seconds now, since that's how long it had taken Venus and Matthew to light it and leave.

You know how I keep referring back that conversation Min, Gunnar, and I had at the zoo, the start of that whole Elephant of Surprise thing?

This is the part where I even surprised myself.

The fuse kept burning, hissing in the night as the fire snaked its way closer to the explosives. As the light flickered ever closer to its destination, I saw the dynamite itself for the first time—a whole stack of sticks duct-taped to the side of the water tower, all of them somehow connected to a single fuse. I expected them to be red, but they weren't: they looked beige, at least in the darkness.

"Go!" I said to Wade. "Before the police get here!"

And then I ran toward the dynamite. I didn't consciously think: I need to save that homeless family down below. I don't remember making any kind of decision at all. If I'd *had* an actual choice, I think I might have chosen the cowardly option—or the *sane* one, depending on how you look at it. But instead, I found myself running, past the chain-link fence, through the open door, and into the fenced-off area.

The fuse to the dynamite was still a snake, and I knew it could strike at any second. By the time I was near enough to see it up close, the spark was only inches from the explosive. I hadn't really seen how long the fuse was to begin with, so I didn't know how much time I had left, but I knew it wasn't much.

Even now, I didn't think, didn't hesitate: I just reached out and wrapped my hand around the fuse.

What the hell was I doing? Why wasn't I running away? I said I was liking all the adventure in my life lately, but this was ridiculous!

The snake-like fuse stopped hissing at last. I could also smell the scent of burning flesh, but at least I didn't *feel* it burn.

But I did feel something else. The fuse wasn't

dead: the spark was still alive in my hand, crawling out of my clenched fist like a hard-shelled insect, impossible to crush. The fuse was made of gunpowder, I knew, and gunpowder was made to burn.

I squeezed harder, but it still skittered forward against my skin.

Finally realizing I couldn't squeeze the fuse dead —duh!—I jerked on it, yanking it out, pulling it free. For a second, the gun powder kept sizzling in my hand, but now it didn't have any way to get to the dynamite. The explosives were dead. (In my defense, all this happened in about an eighth of a second!)

At the same time, flashlight beams sliced the misty undergrowth, and voices barked out in the dark. The police had arrived.

Only now did I feel the burn.

Boy, did I feel the burn! My hand throbbed like nothing I'd ever felt before, like I'd just jammed my hand in the toaster.

As the police got closer, I looked around the grass for Wade, but he was gone.

It was very complicated trying to explain to the police that I wasn't the one who had set and lit the dynamite: I was the one who had *stopped* it. But I had the burn-mark on my hand to prove it. And it wasn't long before Min and Gunnar arrived, both out of breath from running through the woods and up the hill, and

Min was able to say that she was the one who had called 9-1-1, and Gunnar was able to explain that he was the one who'd suspected the freegans were planning to blow something up in the first place. It helped that he had the evidence on his phone—although he had to explain it about six times before anyone even had a clue what he was talking about (not Gunnar's fault for once: these police officers seemed unusually dim).

At one point, an officer said, "The metal in that tower is pretty thick. I doubt that dynamite would've been strong enough to blow a hole in the water tower anyway."

And I didn't say anything, but what I wanted to say was: "Is that right? Well, fuck you, you fucking fuck fuck!" Because even if it hadn't blown a hole in that water tower, I was pretty damn sure it would have blown a hole in me!

Eventually, the police took me to the police station, and my parents, who I'd already called, joined me there. Min, Gunnar, and I had to answer a whole bunch more questions, and by then the local media had arrived, so we did interviews with the newspaper and even one of the television stations from a nearby city.

At one point, Gunnar pulled me aside and said, "By the way, I think I'm finally done chronicling my whole life online. But aren't you glad I did?"

I couldn't deny it.

Finally, well after midnight, after all the excitement had died down, my parents took me home. It was easy enough to convince them the freegans were people I hardly knew (which was true), that I'd met them at school with Min and Gunnar (which was also true), and that I'd only been to their house very briefly one single time (which, unfortunately, wasn't true at all).

But I didn't stay at home. Once I was sure my parents were in bed, I crawled out my bedroom window and used my own bike to ride off into the night. There was somewhere I still needed to be, someone I really needed to talk to. And I knew exactly where I'd find him.

I found Wade's bike parked in the bushes outside the abandoned warehouse, the same place where we'd left our bikes once before. I'd been sure he'd be waiting for me here, and I'd been right. I knew he couldn't go back to the freegan house, not now, and the only other place where he'd think to wait for me—the abandoned streetcar in the woods—was too close to the water tower and the police.

It was dark outside. I took the light from my bike, then fumbled my way over to the boarded-up door in the side of the building. The gravel in the parking lot skittered under my feet.

Wade had left the boards undone: he was waiting for me inside. I put my light to one side, then crawled in through the opening—and of course, I forgot all about the pigeon poop and/or bat guano dried onto the floor, so I put my hands right in it all over again.

Once inside, I stood up again. I cleaned my hands on my pants—my one hand still hurt from the burn of the fuse—and shone my light around in the dark. The rusted cans and plastic sheets strewn around the warehouse floor seemed different now, blended in with the pigeon poop and/or bat guano, looking like ripples and waves on a frozen sea. The air smelled different now too, colder and wetter, already filled with a hint of morning dew.

"Wade?" I called, a loud whisper.

The floor creaked, and a shadow stepped out of the little office on the far side of the room. I aimed my light his way, and caught a flash of the crisp white t-shirt peeking out from under his jacket.

I crossed over to him, the dried pigeon poop and/or bat guano crunching under my feet.

I stopped about ten feet in front of the office. I didn't shine the light in his face, but off to one side, so as not to blind him. He stood in the doorway, silently watching me.

"There's one thing I really need to know," I said. "And I need you to be totally honest. Did you really not know about any of this? I don't mean about the water tower. I mean about E.L.F. and eco-terrorism and all the rest."

It was a fair question, and he knew it.

"I didn't," he said. "I'd never do anything like that."

He started toward me, out of the office, but I immediately backed away, so he stopped. I just stared at him. The burn on my hand throbbed.

"No," he said. "I swear to God!" When I kept staring at him, he said, "Russel, you know me. You know I'd never do anything like that."

I finally decided he was telling the complete truth. Relief flooded through me. How could I have ever believed otherwise?

Wade turned away. He walked back to the doorway of the office, leaned against the frame as if for support.

"But," he said.

Great, I thought. Another "but." The beam of light quivered in my hand.

He looked back at me. "Russel, I *should* have known. Gunnar picked it up just from a bunch of pictures he took! I mean, I knew they were planning things, had done things, but I thought it was, like, graffiti on an overpass. They knew I don't go for stuff like that, so that's why I thought they were keeping it from me. I had no idea they'd do anything like this. But I guess part of me didn't *want* to believe it. So I looked the other way. I was so stupid."

"It's not your fault that you look for the best in people," I said. "That you give people the benefit of the doubt." I took a couple of crunchy steps toward him.

But Wade backed away again, all the way into the office.

"Russel, you don't understand. This is all my fault."

Now I was confused. "But you just said you didn't know anything about the plan."

"But all the stupid things Venus heard me say. You don't think that had an impact? What if you hadn't caught them? People could have died. I'm so, so sorry!"

I didn't say anything. He had a point. He wasn't responsible for her actions, but maybe he should've seen it coming. Even so, I couldn't blame him. How could he know what someone else would do? And we all make mistakes. He wasn't perfect just like I wasn't perfect. In a way, this all made my feelings for him that much stronger. It was like, well, a busted water tower, flooding my heart.

"I'm sorry I suspected you," I said. "That was wrong."

Now he didn't say anything. He started pacing back and forth in that little office. There was no pigeon poop and/or bat guano in there, but the floor creaked again.

I stepped into the doorway of the office, watching him. "What is it?"

"Russel, I've been lying to you."

I stiffened. "Wait. What? Are you saying you *were* involved?"

He shook his head. "No, no, not about that. I'm telling the truth about that. It's about something else entirely."

I didn't say anything, just watched him and listened.

"I'm not in love with you."

"Hold on. Who said anything about love? We just met two weeks ago." I was moony-eyed, but even I wasn't that much of a twelve-year-old girl.

"That's not what I mean. I'm not gay." And before I could even think it, he added, "Or bisexual. I'm straight."

I wasn't sure what to think about this. It was a surprise for sure. This conversation wasn't going how I thought it would.

"When did you realize this?" I said.

"I didn't have to realize it. I've always known it."

Now I was really confused. I just stared at him from that doorway. My hand burned with heat.

"I knew you were gay, almost from the beginning," he said. "And I figured you were into me."

"It's okay," I said. "I mean, you met someone you had a connection with, and you were confused. It happens. It's all right." In a way, it even made sense. I mean, if some guys are "questioning" when it comes to being gay, it stood to reason that at least a few of them would decide: well, no, I'm not. Feelings could be confusing, and "questioning" meant just that. It really, really sucked that Wade wasn't into me the way I was into him, but what was I going to do about it? I wouldn't want him to be with me if he didn't love me back. (My heart didn't believe those words, and probably never would, but my head did.)

"Russel, you still don't understand. I was never confused. I never wondered if I was gay."

I felt the light lower in my hand so the beam was pointed down, spilling out around my feet like my whole body was melting like a stick of butter. So much for things making sense.

"I don't get it," I said. "If you weren't confused, why did you say you were?"

"You were just so perfect," he said, pacing nervously again. "The other freegans? They're great people, some of them. But they're drop-outs—rebels or nonconformists. They do things just to shock people, to get a reaction, just like you said. Either that or they're anarchists, like Venus and Matthew—people who've given up on change and just want to blow things up. None of them are going to change the world, not the way it needs to be changed." He looked up at me. "But you were different. You and your friends, Min and Gunnar? You're exactly the kind of people freeganism needs."

"You were pretending to like me just because you wanted to recruit me to your cause?" That broken water tower spilling love into my heart? It had stopped flowing. And any of the love that happened to be still lying around, slowly soaking into my heart? It dried up pretty fast. Suddenly, it was a parched, cracked desert in my heart.

"I *do* like you!" Wade said. "I liked you from the first moment I met you. But..." He'd stopped pacing now, was just staring at me. "I never liked you the way you liked me."

"Just how far would you have taken it?"

"I'm not sure. But I think pretty far."

His clean white t-shirt was still visible from the front of his jacket. Yes, the gay stereotypes were sometimes right, but I guess they were sometimes wrong too. Wade was and always had been straight. It made total sense. The hesitation I'd always sensed in him? It wasn't because he was closeted—it was just him working up the nerve to kiss a guy when he didn't really want to. Or maybe it was a flicker of his conscience, telling him what a shitty thing he was doing. Either way, the Elephant of Surprise was once again rumbling back into my life, destroying everything around it, including my ego. I remembered that morning in the school hallway when Min and Gunnar had accused me of tempting fate by my forsaking love. Gunnar had predicted that fate would punish me by making me fall in love with an ice sculpture. He'd said, "Not only can it not love you back, it'll melt in a couple of hours anyway." That was actually a pretty spot-on description of my relationship with Wade.

I'll do what I have to do to change the world, he'd told me. *Whatever it takes—anything at all.*

Talk about unspoken passions. Maybe he wasn't willing to blow up water towers, but he was more than willing to dupe stupid gay boys into falling in love with him. He'd told me so outright.

"You wanted Min and Gunnar and me," I said. "But I was the only one dumb enough to fall for you."

"No!" Wade said, and the floor whined under his feet. "Russel, it wasn't like that."

"Then how was it?" Something occurred to me. I pointed to the metal locker behind him, the one filled with all his possessions. "Was I really the first person you'd ever showed that to? And the streetcar in the woods?" I'd been so touched both times that Wade was supposedly sharing parts of himself he'd never shown to anyone else.

He hesitated.

The light from my bike slipped from my hand. It hit the floor with a clunk and went out, but I didn't care. Light or not, I was stumbling around in the dark either way.

"I knew it," I said. "It was all an act." I'd actually considered giving up college to go away and live as a freegan! Has there ever been a bigger fool in the history of the world?

"No!" he said. "Russel, you *are* the only one. I've never told anyone else about this locker or that streetcar, I swear to God."

"Then why did you hesitate?"

"Because I knew at the time why I was doing those

things, why you'd think I was doing them. That I was manipulating you. I knew that, and I did it anyway."

Part of me was still furious. But another part of me sensed he was finally telling me the complete truth. That was something, I guess. At least it was kind of flattering that he thought enough of me that he was so eager to recruit me to his cause.

I snorted.

"What?" Wade said, cautious, fearful that I was about to lash out at him.

But I didn't. Instead, I said, "I don't know. I've had people try to manipulate me before in order to get into my pants. But you're the first who's ever tried to get into my brain."

Wade smiled in the moonlight that shone down from the row of windows up by the ceiling. "I think I wish I *was* gay, Russel, because you're a pretty great guy."

Part of me was flattered, even as another part of me wondered if Wade was just trying to manipulate me again.

"No," I said. "If you're going to be friends with a gay guy, that's *exactly* the kind of thing you can't say to him."

He looked at me warily. "*Am* I going to be friends with a gay guy?"

"I don't know," I said, and it was the truth. Wade had done something inexcusable. On the other hand, he'd had his reasons. And I'd done a few inexcusable things in my life too. Or was I just being another moony-eyed gay boy, determined to excuse everything about the straight guy I was secretly still in love with?

No. The love I'd felt for him—the stuff that had been gushing into my heart, but had then dried up? It was long gone. But my heart wasn't a desert exactly. At some point, I needed to decide if what had been growing there could ever come back to life—if anything Wade and I had shared had been real. But there wasn't time for that now.

"What are you going to do?" I said to him. My hand was barely throbbing now.

"What do you think I should do?"

"Leave town," I said. "Tomorrow morning. The police won't understand. No one will understand. They'll think you were involved. And the only way you could ever convince them otherwise is if you hire a really good lawyer—and I don't think you have money for that." This was the one good thing about being a freegan: he *could* leave. Even I didn't know his last name. And I doubted his name was on any lease or bills or anything. Wade could hop a train or catch a ride and be gone in an hour.

"But freeganism is going to get some really bad press in the days ahead," he said. "It's going to get really ugly."

"That's going to happen no matter what. And how are you going to counter what they're saying if you're in jail? I'm serious, Wade. You need to go. Leave now." I dug into my wallet and gave him all the money I had—which, unfortunately, was less than twenty dollars. Then I nodded to the locker. "I promise I'll keep an eye on your stuff. It'll be here for you when you come back." I backed away from the doorway, indicating that I was serious, that he really did need to leave town A.S.A.P.

"Russel, I'm really, really sorry. About everything." He stepped into the doorway of the office and hesitated. But he didn't try to hug me or anything, and I appreciated that (mostly). Instead, he turned toward the exit.

"Keep in mind," I said, stopping him. "I happen to have some friends who are pretty good at communicating. And it just so happens that one of them is the very guy who spotted the E.L.F. plot in the first place. I have a feeling Gunnar'll put in a good word or two for freeganism."

"And then there's the guy who was smart and brave enough to figure it out and actually stop it," Wade said.

For a second, I was confused. Did he mean me? It's funny how I'd already forgotten what I'd done earlier in the night, how I was something of a hero—at least in a certain light and from a certain angle. I had the burn on my hand to prove it.

"I thought I could be the one to teach you all these important things," Wade said. "Turns out you were the one who taught me."

With that, he disappeared into the darkness, and I let myself smile at last.

CHAPTER SIXTEEN

"Well," I said to Min after I'd explained everything, "I made a complete fool out of myself yet again. How many times is that now?"

It was the next day, Tuesday. My parents had let me skip school and sleep in. After all, I'd been up most of the night—even later than my parents thought—and I was supposedly a hero too. But when I'd finally woken up, I'd really needed to talk about what had happened with Wade, so I'd ridden my bike over to Min's. Unlike me, she'd gone to school and come back already.

"Russel," she said to me, "you have nothing to be embarrassed about. Well, except maybe those pants."

"No, think about it," I said. I was pacing while she sat on the bed. "Last year, I pulled that stupid crap with Brian Bund. Then I go to summer camp and fall for that idiot Web. Then I almost let Kevin back into my life, only to discover at the very last second what a jerk he is. And now I have a completely made-up love affair with Wade. I am an absolute idiot! And what's wrong with these pants?" They were light blue cargo pants.

"You're not an idiot."

"Tell me how I'm not an idiot. And oh, God, Gunnar was right—I did tempt fate with all that talk about forsaking love! When Gunnar understands life better than you do, you know you've got a big, big problem."

"Please. You and I should both know by now that Gunnar is operating on a much higher plane of understanding than either of us."

Okay, so maybe Min was right about Gunnar. But she was still wrong about the rest of it. And she was definitely wrong about me not being an idiot. (But now that I took a good look at them, she may have been right about the cargo pants.)

"Russel," Min said, "there's something I need to tell you about Kevin—something you really, really need to know."

"Min, I know you're trying to cheer me up, but there's nothing you can tell me about that jerk that can—"

"He's not a jerk. Trust me when I say that Kevin Land is the exact opposite of a jerk."

What was she going on about? "Min—"

"Just listen, okay? He was only pretending to be a jerk. He's been trying to make you think he's a jerk so that you could forget about him and move on with Otto."

I stared at her.

Min kept talking, and suddenly the planet exploded, and the sun winked out, and gravity stopped working, and our entire solar system was sucked into a big black hole.

No, seriously: everything I thought about the world, everything I assumed I could count on, was blown to pieces.

Min explained how Kevin really had been in love with me last fall—that he really had come out of the closet for my sake, and he'd paid a real price. He'd absolutely wanted me to take him back.

But then Min had laid into him, told him that it had been Kevin's own fault our relationship hadn't worked out the first time around (which was true), that I had a great new boyfriend now, Otto, and that I deserved a chance to try to make it work with him. And Kevin had finally agreed with her.

Kevin hadn't been hooking up with someone else the night I'd gone to meet him at that park. It had been Min I'd seen him with, wearing Leah's overcoat—I'd mistaken her in the dark. Kevin and Min had been hugging, because Kevin had been crying, realizing that he and I couldn't be together anymore—that Min was right, and he needed to let me move on. And when I'd confronted Kevin, accused him of hooking up with older guys in the park, he hadn't corrected me. No, he'd played along, letting me jump to conclusions, pretending to be a total jerk, just so I would finally have him out of my system once and for all, so I could finally, truly be with Otto.

When she was done, I didn't say anything. I was too stunned. Also, the Earth no longer existed, so there wasn't any oxygen left to breathe anyway.

Finally, I choked something out. "But what about the thing with Brian Bund? And his fight with Ben?"

"I don't know," Min said. "Maybe that was real—none of us is perfect. Or maybe he staged that too."

But even as Min said it, I knew that that's exactly what had happened. He had seen me see him with Brian Bund, laughing in the library, and he must have realized I had Gunnar watching him too. He couldn't have me realizing he wasn't a monster, so he'd gotten Brian to pretend to have a fight with him just so Gunnar could see it and report back to me what a jerky person he was. And he'd done the same thing with Ben.

But if that thing with Ben had been staged, that meant Kevin would've had to know my schedule, to know I'd be walking across that little courtyard right then. And that meant he'd had to have *observed* me. Had he been watching me all along the way I'd been watching him? This made perfect sense if he still loved me the way Min said he did.

I could hardly believe someone had done all these cool things for another person, made all these incredible sacrifices. It was even harder to believe that someone had done all these things for me. But Kevin had.

For me. Kevin really did love me. He'd made his mistakes—hey, we all had. But unlike most of the other nine billion people on the planet, he was actively trying to make amends for them.

Talk about the Elephant of Surprise! But this time, he wasn't stomping on my head. This time, I was riding on his back, in one of those Indian saddle-like seat-contraptions, with the little tasseled awnings. He was carrying me down the mountain at a healthy clip, a victorious return.

I noticed Min staring at me, her forehead furrowed.

Suddenly, I was angry—not just at myself. At Min. I thought I'd been in the wilderness of romance with someone, that I'd been connected to her on this deep, metaphysical level, but it turns out I'd been all alone after all.

"Why didn't you tell me this before?" I said.

"Russel, I'm really sorry. I guess I was so caught up in the thing with Leah that I sort of forgot all about it. But I did *try* to tell you. Remember? Weeks ago? I tried again just yesterday. But you insisted you didn't want to hear. You said there was absolutely nothing I could say that would make you want to talk to Kevin."

I did have a memory of her saying something like

that. But I hadn't known what I was talking about! Who wouldn't want to know *this*? It changed everything!

But I couldn't stay mad at Min. Now I was just angry at myself. What had I done? Why hadn't I listened when Min had tried to tell me the truth?

"I need to talk to him," I said to Min. "Do you think he'll talk to me?"

"You can always try." She pointed to her computer which was already on. I'd slept in so long it was now late in the afternoon. Kevin could be home from school by now—he could even be home from baseball practice.

I logged in and IMed Kevin (screen name: Lando14). I said I needed to see him, that I had something I needed to tell him.

Lando14: Fuck off!

I stared at those words on my computer screen. I now knew just how much love was contained in that simple "Fuck off!" Have there ever been two more romantic words in the history of the universe? It was all I could do not to cry.

Smuggler: This is really important. I'll be waiting at the stinky picnic gazebo in 15 minutes. Please come.

I logged off right after that, and I turned off my phone too. Maybe I couldn't make Kevin show up, but I could at least stop him from *telling* me he wasn't coming. For some reason, that gave me a feeling of control.

"Good luck," Min said. For the second time in two days, and the second time since I'd known her, there were tears in her eyes.

I rode my bike to the place where I'd told Kevin to meet me, the stinky picnic gazebo. Just so you know, it's nothing like the gazebo in that scene where Julie Andrews meets Christopher Plummer in *The Sound of Music* (that's what I would think). For one thing, this gazebo is in a park that's located next to a swamp, so the methane smell is just ridiculous. That's why no one ever goes there, for picnics or anything. But that meant it had been the perfect place to first meet Kevin, back when we'd both been closeted. It was also the place where, eight months later, he'd pretended to be hooking up with someone so I would get angry and reject him.

Kevin wasn't there, so I waited. Was he even going to come? Kevin's house wasn't any farther from the gazebo than Min's.

After all the times I'd come here at night, it was strange to be here just after dusk, to watch the long shadows of the afternoon slowly blend into darkness.

I waited for a long time, but I wasn't about to leave. That would be the same as turning on my phone to see that he'd texted me to say he wasn't coming. No, the only control I had now was staying right where I was.

"Russel."

I turned. Kevin had somehow come upon me from behind. He looked smaller than I remembered, but also more solid. More real.

"Don't tell me to fuck off," I said. "Don't say anything. I know the truth about what you've been doing, and why. I made Min tell me everything she knew, and I figured out the rest."

"I know," he said. "I had a feeling that's why you contacted me, so I called her myself." So *that's* why it had taken him so long to get here.

"I can't believe you did all that!" I said. "Making me hate you so I could be with Otto?"

Kevin didn't confirm or deny anything. He didn't say anything at all—wouldn't even look me in the eye. He just stared off into the gathering night.

"I do love Otto," I said. "In a very real way, I always will. But not the way I thought I did. As a friend. We broke up a couple of weeks ago."

Kevin nodded. "I had a feeling. I've been following Gunnar's posts."

Kevin was following Gunnar online too? I guess I'd been really wrong when I'd said no one was reading his posts. Still, it made sense. This was even better than having one of his friends spy on me: he had one of *my own friends* spying on me.

Remember when Min had told me the truth about Kevin and I'd said the planet had been sucked into a black hole, and gravity and air had all disappeared? It was all back now, stronger than ever. The earth had never felt so solid. I stepped forward and kissed him, breathing him in—he still smelled like leather from a baseball mitt and dollar soap. I didn't care who saw us: I'd kiss him in the shopping mall if I could. So much had changed in the last year, since the very first time we'd agreed to meet at this gazebo, when we hadn't even known each other's names—only that we went to each other's school. I didn't feel like a spy lurking in the shadows now, or an outsider, or a fraud.

Kevin kissed me back. Boy, did he kiss me back! I was a guy who loved another guy, and that guy loved me back even if I was wearing truly horrible blue cargo pants. Maybe this was like that gazebo in *The Sound of Music* after all, except with hot guy-on-guy action. It didn't matter that I'd tempted fate those weeks before—I was getting my happy ending anyway. This was the biggest surprise of all. Was it because I'd been a hero back at the water tower—because I'd saved that woman and her kid? (Turns out they'd been there after all.) I still had my issues with fate, but now at least I knew it—she?—played fair.

But something was wrong. When I'd kissed Wade, I'd realized how good it felt to kiss a smile, but Kevin wasn't smiling now. He was crying. That didn't feel so good.

I pulled back.

"What is it?" I said.

He turned away.

"Kevin?"

"I'm scared," he said. Sure enough, his shoulders quivered.

"What?" I said. "Why?" Now he was scaring *me*. Didn't he want to be together now?

He rubbed his eyes. "Because I'm finally getting what I wanted. And I'm not sure I could stand to lose it again."

I smiled, relieved. "You won't lose it. You won't lose me."

He faced me again. "You don't know that. You *can't* know that. Neither of us can."

And suddenly I saw what Kevin was getting at. He was absolutely right. Maybe Kevin and I would stay together this time, maybe we wouldn't. Who knew what would happen in a week or a month or a year? Who knew how I would feel—or how *he* would feel? If I'd learned anything these past few weeks, it was that Min had been right: I couldn't predict the future. No one could. That was the whole point of the Elephant of Surprise. And that damn elephant was never going away. He was as much a part of life as the air we breathe—air that was still reeking of methane, by the way.

Right then I realized something about the Elephant of Surprise, something I hadn't ever thought of before. I'd always thought of the elephant as a bad thing. But maybe it wasn't. It's not just that the elephant's surprises were sometimes good—like now, learning just how much Kevin had loved me all these months. It's that the Elephant of Surprise made life *interesting*. With that elephant around, you never knew what was going to happen next. That had been the problem in my relationship with Otto—the elephant had left the circus.

I tried to explain all this to Kevin, but I'm not sure he understood. It didn't matter. We had so much else to talk about.

We stayed together at that gazebo for a long time, kissing some, but mostly sitting on the steps, just holding hands and talking. I did make a point to text my parents and tell them I was going to spend the night with Gunnar—I figured they couldn't complain after my being such a hero the day before, and I was right.

Kevin and I kept talking, sometimes laughing and sometimes even crying again. I didn't notice the cold, and after a while, I couldn't even smell the methane from the swamp anymore. But I could still smell Kevin.

At one point, he saw something out in the mist that had gathered above the grass in the playfield next to the gazebo. The fog wasn't swirling or moving at all—it was completely frozen, a snapshot of a dark smear stretched across the horizon.

"What is it?" I said.

He pointed. A faint yellow light glowed on the other side of that mist like a light bulb through a blanket.

He laughed. "It's morning. We talked the whole night through!"

"Yeah," I said, taking Kevin's hand. I didn't say what I was really thinking, which was that it wasn't just morning on the other side of the mist—it was the future, wild and unpredictable. But we couldn't see it, not hidden behind all that frozen grey.

Thing is, that didn't scare me, not at all. On the contrary, suddenly I couldn't wait for it to begin.

ABOUT THE AUTHOR

Brent Hartinger is the author of many books, mostly for and about teenagers. *Geography Club*, the first book in the Lambda Award-winning Russel Middlebrook Series, has been adapted into a successful stage play and a feature film starring Scott Bakula and Nikki Blonsky. Brent was also the co-founder of the website AfterElton.com, which was sold to Viacom/MTV in 2006. Read more by and about Brent, or contact him at brenthartinger.com.

ALSO BY BRENT HARTINGER

The Russel Middlebrook Series

Geography Club (Book 1)
The Order of the Poison Oak (Book 2)
Double Feature: Attack of the Soul-Sucking Brain Zombies/Bride of the Soul-Sucking Brain Zombies (Book 3)
The Elephant of Surprise (Book 4)

Other Books

The Last Chance Texaco
Grand & Humble
Project Sweet Life
Shadow Walkers

ACKNOWLEDGEMENTS

It's a cliché to say that words can't express the gratitude I feel to the following individuals regarding this book, but I'm saying it anyway, because it's true: my loyal agent Jennifer DeChiara; my prophetic editor Steve Fraser; my faithful partner Michael Jensen; my cheering squad Tom Baer, Tim Cathersal, Lori Grant, Sarah Jellen, Marcy Rodenborn, and James Venturini; and my very patient early readers Brian Katcher, Frank Anthony Polito, and Frederick Levy.

Made in the USA
Charleston, SC
26 January 2013